Aggie,

You are a master

of Antinning Sillways!

Robert

7/16/11

Swim SidewayZ

Living and Learning Through the Strong Currents of Life and Business

by

Dr. Robert Watts, Jr.

WATTS & ASSOCIATES

Swim SidewayZ

Copyright © 2010 by Dr. Robert Watts Jr.

Requests for information should be addressed to:
Watts & Associates
P.O. Box 0755, Clovis, CA 93612
www.wattsassociates.org

*Library of Congress Cataloging-in-Publication
Data available upon request.
ISBN 978-1-4507-5504-7*

*Printed in the United States of America
April 2011*

*Swim SidewayZ: Leading and Learning
Through the Strong Currents of Life and Business*

Published by Watts and Associates
P.O. Box 0755, Clovis, CA 93612-0755

DEDICATION

Swim SidewayZ is dedicated to one of my best friends and chief cheerleader, Dr. DaSharoi Crocker, of Fresno, California; she was a central source of inspiration during the writing of this book.

In particular, the courage and innovation she modeled in navigating through the tough currents of her cancer diagnosis and treatments, while simultaneously managing two part-time jobs and earning her doctorate in organizational development, exemplifies the character of the protagonist in Swim SidewayZ.

ACKNOWLEDGMENTS

SPECIAL THANKS TO:

Byron Hemingway, my brother-in-Christ, for all his spiritual support and friendship.

Colita Hudson, my friend, for cheering me on and giving me feedback on the first draft of the manuscript.

Dennis Jeffrey, my brother-in-Christ, printer, and friend.

Erika Watts, my daughter, for reading and offering her unbiased feedback on the first drafts of the manuscript.

Greg F. Stewart, my friend of over thirty years, for reviewing the first chapters of the manuscript and encouraging me to complete it.

Jeremiah E. Watts, my son, for reviewing the manuscript and providing me feedback.

John Costen, my brother, for being a model of courage and innovation.

Jolly and Rhonda Kumar, my nephew and niece, for their love and belief in me.

Connie Connor, my big sister, for being a surrogate mother and a standard-bearer of our late mother's love.

Willie Young, my big brother, for being a tower of strength and confidence.

Mike Leonardo, my dear friend and client, for extending himself by reading my manuscript and offering extensive written feedback on evenings and weekends, away from his job, as the director of a large public utilities department.

Robert Watts, III, my son, and namesake for assisting in the development of the life-saving technique of swimming sideways out of ocean currents, as metaphor for leading and managing through life and business, and for his feedback on the first drafts of the manuscript.

Dr. Shelley Stokes, my friend and physician, for sharing his insight and passion for learning, and for taking the time to read Swim SidewayZ and provide valuable feedback.

CONTENTS

INTRODUCTION

My life has been a marvelous journey, whether navigating through life's currents formed by cancer, thyroid disease, parental abdication, or a professional athletic career truncated by debilitating injuries. I count them all joyful opportunities to display the gracious gifts of grace, faith, courage, creativity, innovation, forgiveness, and interdependence.

Overcoming my life challenges was possible only because of the miracles performed on my behalf by family, friends, and the many strangers who sojourned with me before continuing on their journeys. I have learned that I could achieve anything if I stayed open to the possibility of miracles.

It is from this perspective that I viewed the economic debacle that imploded in 2008 and pondered how I could use my background as a writer and organizational consultant to make a difference. I looked to nature for a metaphor to illustrate the values gaps in leadership that I believed were central to the problem. After months of review and discussions with clients, colleagues, and family members, I decided to use the powerful force of the ocean's rip currents.

A rip current is an event in nature that appears as a narrow stream in the water after waves break at the shoreline before it returns out to sea. Too often swimmers get caught in these currents and are carried out to sea. This happens because their instincts and ignorance of how to survive the experience lead to them to approach the problem by panicking and swimming harder into the current, which eventually exhausts them and ends in their demise. Upon learning this, I wondered whether there was a way to survive this experience. I was overjoyed to discover that by turning parallel to the shore and swimming sideways one could free himself from the current.

I thought about the mistakes people make with rip currents and how they represented the approach of too many leaders of organizations. This caused me to carefully study the strategies applied in surviving the experience. After careful observation, I concluded that applying *innovation* was the primary strategy that empowered people to survive the seemingly insurmountable force of the current. The simple technique of maintaining one's composure and swimming sideways out of the current was all that was necessary for success.

Using this knowledge, I wrote the story of Ed Preston, the strong-willed protagonist of Swim SidewayZ. Ed's journey includes his battle against swimming into the currents of leadership practices ill-suited to navigating his company through the strong currents of an economy eroding his company's market share. Receiving help from some special dolphin friends, a loving wife, and a talented and compassionate executive staff, Ed uses composure and innovation to lead his staff in swimming sideways out of the clutches of a poor economy.

Chapter 1

Ed Preston sat in his large office among a cluster of miniature models of windows put in by his residential window installation company. His office was adorned with symbols of his success: a plaque for businessperson of the year, photos of him at his home with star players from his beloved Los Angeles Dodgers and Anaheim Angels, and citations for his local philanthropy. Ed had been a talented baseball player in high school, and his son had spent a couple of years pitching for AA clubs, so being on a first name basis with professional baseball players was important to him. For him, it was a sign of his success.

Ed was the CEO of Preston Window Installations, Inc., a privately held company he had purchased 15 years prior from his former employer, mentor, and surrogate uncle. He had achieved his success the old-fashioned way; he had literally worked his way up from the bottom. Twenty years had passed since Ed bought the company from his uncle, and though the business was still operating in the black, the recent downturn in the US economy troubled him.

Ed's sole customer base was the residential building contractors who subcontracted out window installations to companies like Preston, Inc. Based on the strength of his personality and the reputation of

Preston as a reliable and quality installer, Ed had managed to corner the market among the builders in his community.

He had learned how to install windows as a high school student while working on the construction crew of Hank Sorensen, a World War II friend of his dad. Hank and Ed's dad had become best friends at the veteran's hospital while they were recovering from wounds suffered during the U.S. invasion of Normandy.

Upon returning to civilian life, the friends went into business for themselves. Hank chose to enter the trade taught to him by his father, home construction, while Ed's dad launched his own plumbing operation.

Being best friends, they often worked together on jobs and made it their business to refer each other to potential customers. Hank used a business model that involved using teenage labor as a way of keeping down labor costs. It was also a reliable and available labor pool. Best of all, it helped to serve his altruistic nature since he employed middle and lower income kids as a way of putting money in their pockets and keeping them off the streets during the summer months.

From Hank, Ed also learned the importance of providing quality service and giving back to the communities he served. He, too, employed local teens, sponsored many charitable organizations, and even developed a reputation for helping builders who had fallen on hard times. This was Ed's way of showing people he valued them for more than their work. He developed an ethical persona, and this made him a standout in the contractor's community, where the perception for many was of self-centeredness and unethical practices.

Ed worked for his dad from time to time, but sometimes there wasn't enough work for Ed's dad to pay a crew, or even a helper. Besides, his dad was a solitary person, and following the war he became more introverted and, at times, would withdraw from his wife and son. He preferred working by himself and talking with Hank; he often turned to Hank to talk about the bouts of depression he was still experiencing since the war.

Hank could identify with what Ed's dad was going through, he too had had bouts with post-traumatic stress disorder, but found relief from working with the young people on his crew. He attributed his peace of mind to having the kids around with their carefree attitudes, boundless energy, and penchant for living in the moment. Like Ed's dad, Hank also was a Depression Era teen and never looked past the goal of providing for his immediate needs. The war, as well as the Depression, had taught him to worry about eating for the day, as there was no promise for tomorrow.

He didn't like to look too far into the future, and this included what might be required to sustain his business. He was content with the rise in demand for suburban home construction, created through the issuing of Veteran Administration loans to GIs returning from the war. He had also developed a reputation as a reliable subcontractor among the leading general contractors in the area and was getting a decent share of work. He felt that the demand would surely last until he was ready to retire.

Ed also learned how to take things in stride. His employees perceived him as an even-tempered and easy-to-talk-to problem solver. No matter what the circumstances might be, they could count on Ed to both find a viable solution and keep a smile on his face while doing it. Ed viewed as his duty to keep his people employed and not look to them for help with solving leadership problems.

Preston, Inc. didn't have a functioning board or executive committee; it was a privately held company and Ed and his wife, Anne, were the only board members and shareholders. With the downturn in the market, contracts were drying up and contractors were not calling as often. Ed thought hard about what to do. He maintained the calm, outward demeanor and insulated approach used by the men of his father's and Hank's generation, American war heroes who had saved America from Fascism and Communism, a leadership style that was slow to ask for help or admit weaknesses. He was using a model that seemed to trap him in a cocoon of his own thoughts; he was operating his business using a model that put pressure on him to get the company out of the difficulties it was currently facing. What had worked for Hank in a less complicated business environment during an economic boom in the 50s and 60s, was now working against Ed in 2008.

While Preston had a net worth of 300K, most of it existed in real estate holdings, equipment, work vehicles, inventory, and outstanding accounts receivables. The country was in a colossal real estate collapse. Large institutional banks and mortgage lenders were going out of business or going into receivership. Names like Bear Stearns, Countrywide, Indymac, Fannie Mae, Freddie Mac, AIG, and all the popular automotive manufactures were appearing on the nightly news and in newspapers as casualties of risky lending practices and poor investing.

Because of subprime loans, the nation was witnessing record foreclosures on single-family homes that drove down existing home values. To make matters worse, the price of oil had skyrocketed, driving up gas and diesel prices. This economic sea change significantly affected Ed's business; the lifeblood of his company, new construction, all but came to a halt.

Where business existed, the competition for the few contracts available was fierce. Because there was very little working capital available in the company, Ed, for the first time in his career, faced the possibility of having to cut jobs. He agonized over this to the point of nausea. He loved every one of his people and they him; he had known many of them, especially his installers, since they were teenagers, and some had been with the company since Hank made him a supervisor.

With all of this on his mind, Ed sat at his desk and stared out the window at the ocean in the distance. Watching the waves breaking and crashing was relaxing to him, helping him to get clear about the crux of the problem. He knew that achieving clarity about the problem would be an efficient means of reaching a solution. Consequently, he reflected on the past in order to gain a clear perspective of the present and future. He went in search of a clue by reflecting back on when he first went into business for himself.

After graduating from high school, Ed enrolled at a local college with the intention of majoring in business. He was enjoying college life and had even met someone who would become his best friend for the rest of his life, Anne Jennings.

After completing his first year, Ed called Hank to find out if he needed any help for the summer, and jokingly asked, "Do you have any work for college kids looking to stay out of trouble for the summer?"

Hank said, "Well, it depends on if the college kid isn't afraid to get his hands a little dirty." They both laughed. Hank said it would be fun to have him on the crew for the summer; it would give them a chance to catch up.

Things were going smoothly that summer. Ed was making a little extra money since Hank had increased his pay from the previous summer. Hank considered him a more experienced worker who could lead a crew of high-school kids, and because Hank started his crews out at 6 a.m., he usually stopped working at 3 p.m.; this gave Ed more time to spend with his best friend, Anne.

As the summer ended and Ed was preparing to return to school, he received a frantic call from his mother.

"Ed, Dad was rushed to the hospital; we think he suffered a heart attack at work!" By the time Ed arrived at the hospital his dad had already passed away. He was 62 years old. Ed was distraught that he had not had a chance to say goodbye to his dad. The only thing he could remember was the conversation they had had earlier in the summer. Ed was his only child, so his father asked him to promise that if anything ever happened to him he would take care of his mother. Ed chuckled and assured him that he would do so, that he should never question whether he would look after his mom.

Ed's mother had suffered most of her adult life with chronic neck and back pain caused by an automobile accident, and even found it difficult on most days to tend to her beloved vegetable and rose gardens. Her disability was permanent and prevented her from pursuing a career in nursing. Compounding things was the denial of insurance coverage for Ed's dad because of an underlying heart condition.

His father had been the owner of a small plumbing business and, while they were not rich, he had managed to provide a home and a decent living for his family, but had not invested his money. Ed's dad was a Depression Era teen; he didn't believe in investing in the stock market. Instead, he saved his money in savings and loans institutions, under the mattress, in shoeboxes, and in jelly jars. He had not established a retirement program, but he had paid off the small house they lived in, and their two Buicks.

At the reception, following his dad's funeral, Ed sat at the kitchen table as the guests congregated on the patio to tell stories about his dad. It was clear to Ed that he would have to forego college and find a job. It worried him that he wasn't sure what he could do to earn enough money to take care of himself and his mother.

Hank approached Ed, put his arm around his shoulders, and said, "Kid, you know your father was like a brother to me, so that makes you like a nephew to me." Ed looked up at Hank and smiled.

"Thanks, Uncle Hank." He had never said that to him before, nevertheless, it felt right to say it because it gave him a sense of the security he was seeking. Like each of his parents, he was an only child. There were no uncles or aunts for him to turn to for comfort or guidance. Essentially, he and his mother were in the world by themselves.

"So what are you going to do my boy; I mean when are you going back to college?" Hank said.

"Well, Uncle Hank, I don't think I will be going back immediately; I need to find a job in order to help take care of my mom. She needs money for medication and doctor visits."

"I understand, son. Well, why don't you come back to work with me? Things are going well with the business and I could use your help. I can start up a new crew with your help."

Hank had not planned on expanding the business until that moment. "Well, that would be great Uncle Hank, thanks!"

"No problem, my boy," Hank said as he patted him on the back. "You take a couple of weeks to get things together and call me when you're ready to go to work... Do you need some cash to tide you over until you start?" Hank asked.

"No, but thanks. Dad left us enough cash to get by for a couple of years, so I'm okay ... I'll call you in a couple of weeks," replied Ed.

Ed fast became the best worker his uncle had and after a few years, he made Ed a crew chief. Ed was a model of discipline, efficiency, and attention to detail. His crew outperformed all the other crews by at least 30%. This meant that often they completed jobs a month or two ahead of other crews. At first, his crew bristled against his approach but quickly learned to appreciate its value. It was their attitude that they shouldn't work to make his uncle rich; he was a nice guy who gave them jobs when they needed them, but he wasn't sharing his profits with them.

Recognizing their concern, Ed had approached his uncle and explained to him how he could make more money by paying the crew a percentage of the profits he earned from bringing jobs in on time. He convinced his uncle to allow his crew to assist other crews when they fell behind on projects, this way they would earn additional income, and the company would improve its efficiency. Ed explained that it was his strategy to have them finish jobs ahead of schedule. He said in doing so they could team with crews that were less efficient and help those crews bring contracts in on time or ahead of schedule too.

His crew grew to love working with Ed. The men saw their pay increase by 20%. Now many of them could think about buying a house, starting a college fund, or taking their wives or girlfriends on a nice vacation. He expanded the business by adding more crews, and soon other crews began to recognize the benefit to working more efficiently and stepped up their efforts. These results lead to more net revenue for Ed's uncle and other opportunities to grow the business. Hank credited Ed with the success of the business and, as a reward, offered him an ownership position. Since he didn't have any children to pass the business to, he made Ed a 30% partner and asked him to manage all the crews.

Always seeking ways to create more profits, Ed figured out that he could grow the business even more while reducing its costs by scaling down its core business operations. He believed that the business could make more profit by focusing solely on window installations. He calculated that they could save money by completing more jobs in a shorter period if they lowered their operating costs and subcontracted to mid-sized developers looking to lower their labor and insurance costs. Hank didn't fully understand Ed's business approach, but his intuition told him to trust the kid. After all, he had gone to college for a year and had created more value than he had thought was possible.

Ed put his plan into motion and it didn't take him long to realize that he had made the right decision. The large and mid-sized developers were happy to pass the window installations over to Preston and now they could either downsize their crews, thereby cutting labor costs and/or bid on multiple contracts without the concern of not having available crews. It was a stroke of genius; within a year Preston, Inc. realized a 40% increase in net profits from the previous year. This growth continued at a pace of approximately 1000% for the next ten years. Behind Ed's suggestions and guidance, the business had grown its net worth from 50K to $5 million.

It was at this time that his uncle learned that he was suffering from a rare, debilitating blood disease and, while not fatal, it was chronic and he would require treatment for the rest of his life. It was abundantly clear that he wouldn't be able to meet the demands of a growing business, nor be interested in spending the remainder of his life working. He and his wife had decided to live out their dream of purchasing a large motor home and traveling throughout the United States, Canada, and Mexico.

Recognizing his uncle's predicament and aspiration, and the opportunity to own the business, Ed met with a business consultant. Together they developed a strategy to buy out his uncle's share of the business. The strategy consisted of a $2 million buyout with a 500K payment up front for control of the business. The remainder would be paid over five years with 2% ownership in the business for an additional ten years.

Ed approached his uncle with the offer and his uncle gladly accepted the deal. His only worry was that maybe Ed was getting in over his head a bit. Ed told his uncle not to worry; he had done some scenario analysis and determined that record growth in the real estate sector was going to occur in California, Nevada, and Arizona over the next twenty years and that he was going to expand the business strategically to match the needs of builders in all the western states. Ed did a masterful job of implementing his plan; he grew the business to a net worth of $30 million and employed 100 full-time workers.

Now, with the economy tanking, all that had come to an abrupt end. Ed had noticed the decline for a couple of years, but, committed to the notion that things would turn around, he failed to respond with a different strategy. Anne suggested that he look at diversifying the business, but he was resolute in the idea that the housing market would correct itself and that change was just around the bend. Off by himself, Ed knew that she was right, but he wasn't sure how to diversify the business or service. Ed felt, for obvious reasons, that going back to Hank's original model of small-home construction wasn't the answer. Ed had never thought of another business or doing anything else; installation was what he had immersed himself in for the last 30 years, nothing else interested him.

He had journeyed all the way back to when he started the business but failed to gain any clarity about a strategy to turn the situation around. Ed felt exhausted and anxious; he was clinching his teeth and the back of his neck and shoulders were tense and hard as rocks. Suddenly, he felt like he couldn't catch his breath. He was 58 years old and had not done a great job of staying in shape. Long gone was the 32-inch waist he enjoyed like a high school athlete. He worried that maybe he was experiencing early warning signs of a heart attack; after all, his dad had passed away at the age of 62. Had the stress of the last few years awakened an underlying congenital condition?

Feeling overwhelmed by thoughts of things outside his control, Ed decided to leave the office for his favorite stress-relieving activity. He grabbed his sunglasses and briefcase and, as he sped by onto the elevator, announced to his assistant that he was leaving for the day. She shouted out, "Is everything alright, Ed?" in a concerned voice. Her inquiry seemed to land on deaf ears, as Ed offered no reply. It was 1 p.m. when Ed exited the building; this alarmed his assistant because Ed seldom ended his workday before 6 p.m.

Hopping into his convertible Mercedes Benz, Ed sought refuge from the stress at a private beach owned by a friend. There he could swim without disturbance. Ed loved to swim in the ocean. The sound of the wind and waves, combined with the subtle slapping of his arms against the cold, salty water offered a welcome respite. After forty five minutes of swimming, the reiterative thoughts about the situation at Preston, Inc. had quieted. With his head clear, Ed changed course and headed back towards the beach. After a minute he discovered that instead of drawing closer to the shore he had drifted further away from it.

Panting heavily from exhaustion, he realized his physical condition left a lot to be desired and attributed it to why he wasn't making more progress towards the shore. He took a deep breath, put his face in the water, and swam with all his skill and strength. But thirty seconds later, he had drifted yet further out to sea.

Now feeling anxious and lost in a sea of thoughts about all that could be wrong, Ed's instincts compelled him to try even harder to reach the shore. All he achieved was a greater state of exhaustion and less progress towards achieving his goal. After several minutes of pushing his body to its limits, Ed lifted his head with the hopes of calling out to someone for help, but the beach was deserted. He slapped at the water in a desperate attempt to reach the beach, but with every stroke, he slowly began to succumb to his ill fate.

Exhausted, Ed lost coordination between when he took breaths, made strokes, and accidentally gulped some of the salty water. The momentary loss of breath panicked him and stopped him from swimming.

Now his exhaustion, combined with fear, resigned him to treading water. As he bobbed in the water, he could feel the current pulling him further and further out to sea. Thinking this was the end; he put his head back, looked up at the sky, and cried, believing that he would never see his beloved mother, or Anne, again.

As Ed slowly drifted further out to sea he heard what he thought were the voices of small children, they appeared to be whispering into his ear. Because his ears were under water, he could only surmise that he was hallucinating. Lifting his head out of the water and looking around, Ed could see that a pod of four Bottlenose Dolphins had surrounded him. Each of the animals called out for him to "Swim SidewayZ."

Ed, convinced that he was losing touch with reality, put his head back and began floating on his back. Sensing Ed's disbelief, the dolphins persisted vehemently by slapping the water with their flippers and pleading in high-pitched screams, "Please Swim SidewayZ! Please ... please Swim SidewayZ!" Nevertheless, their pleas were to no avail. Ed was no longer listening to what he believed was his hallucinations.

The dolphins, determined not to lose Ed to the sea, used the tops of their heads to turn him parallel to the shore, nudging him forward and across the strong currents. As they pushed Ed clear of the currents, they used their beaks to turn Ed towards the beach and escorted him safely to the shallows. Ed staggered to shore. They had saved his life.

As Ed lay collapsed on the beach, he could hear the dolphins calling out to him. Summoning what little strength he had he sat up to see the dolphins skipping backwards on their fluke fins. As he watched them, they called out to him in unison, "Remember to Swim SidewayZ out of danger! Swim SidewayZ to break bad habits! Swim SidewayZ to get ahead!"

Ed thought he had lost his mind, but he was so grateful to be alive that he waved to the dolphins and yelled, "Thank you!" to them as they somersaulted high into the air and then plunged into the sea and disappeared.

The near-death experience shook Ed; he wasn't sure whether he had experienced what had taken place. He felt the tension of a paradox raging within him. He wasn't someone who was open to the possibility of miracles; if a thing couldn't be supported by science, he didn't believe in it. He knew that dolphins couldn't speak English, so to solve the problem he deduced that maybe he had passed out from the near drowning and had somehow been washed ashore by the strong current. He couldn't accept the fact that a school of dolphins rescued him, but, on the other hand, he was a pragmatist at heart. Therefore, if it led to a practical end, maybe it was possible. To think so would mean that he had lost touch with reality. For the moment, he decided to be saved by waves was probably the sane conclusion. However, he thought to himself, "But, I had said thank you and waved goodbye to the imaginary dolphins."

Shaken by the ordeal, Ed could barely make the 20-minute drive home. Several times he felt overcome with anxiety and thought of pulling off onto the median. Yet, he was anxious to talk of his experience with the person he trusted the most, his wife of 20 years. So with trembling hands, he meandered through the winding, palm-lined streets of the small coastal town of white-washed houses and red Adobe roofs. He stumbled into the house, spent from the experience, and looked pale from the fear that he would never see Anne again.

"Ed, is that you, Honey?" Anne called out in a startled voice. It was unusual for Ed to come home in the middle of the day. When Anne saw Ed standing in the mudroom, she grew alarmed by his appearance. "Dear, are you okay, what happened? You look as if you've seen a ghost." Before he could answer, she asked, "Are you coming down with something?" feeling his forehead with the back of her hand.

"No," he replied trying to mask his distress, "just a pool of dolphins."

His attempts were in vain, after twenty years of being his best friend, Anne knew that something had deeply shaken Ed. She likened his appearance to the ashen face he wore the day he learned that his father had passed.

Anne moved closer to Ed and carefully took his shaking hands in hers and asked him in a tender voice to tell her what was bothering him and about the dolphins. After summoning the courage, Ed told Anne the whole story, then waited for her to call the people with the white jackets. He told her that he was seriously concerned that maybe he had lost his mind, that maybe all he was going through at Preston, Inc. had finally taken a toll on him. To his surprise, Anne shared a news event with him that assured him he wasn't delusional.

"Give me a second, Sweetie; I want to read something to you," she said affectionately. She rushed into the den and retrieved a newspaper from the credenza that she ironically had added to her newspaper and magazine journal a couple of months ago. It was a story about a school of dolphins that saved a surfer from an attack by a Great White shark off the Southern California Coastline.

The article discussed how on its first attack on the surfer, the shark had bit a chunk of flesh from the surfer's quadriceps muscles in an attempt to immobilize him. Remarkably, in spite of his injuries, the surfer made a desperate and frantic beeline for the shore as the shark circled back and angled for its second, and likely fatal, bite. As it closed in for the attack, the pod of dolphins intercepted the shark and bombarded it with sonar, driving it off. The part of the article that most captured Ed's attention was the part that spoke of how the dolphins had pushed the surfer to shore where his fellow surfers could assist him. It mirrored the heroics of the pod that had saved his life.

When Anne finished reading the article, Ed collapsed on the sofa with tears streaming down his face. Anne consoled him with a hug, "Honey, see, you were not imagining the dolphins, and you are not losing your mind."

Ed sat there rigidly in Anne's arms and said, "What does it all mean—I mean, what's the likelihood that I would be saved from drowning by a pod of dolphins?"

"Well, my grandmother said when things like that happen to someone it means that there is some purpose that he must fulfill in his life—that his contribution to his generation isn't complete," Anne said philosophically.

"Well, that might be true, but how does someone ever discover what his purpose is or what his contribution needs to be?" Ed asked pensively.

As Ed reflected on his experience with the dolphins, he recalled their admonishment to him, "Remember to Swim SidewayZ out of danger! Swim SidewayZ to break bad habits! Swim SidewayZ to get ahead!" The echoing words in Ed's head relaxed him as he returned Anne's hug.

Chapter 2

Ed tossed and turned throughout the night with the message from the dolphins reverberating in his head, "Swim SidewayZ out of danger! Swim SidewayZ to break bad habits! Swim SidewayZ to get ahead!" He was curious about the significance of Swimming SidewayZ, in particular. Why were the dolphins pronouncing it with the letter "Z?" Moreover, he pondered why they urged him to do it.

Half-awake, Ed rolled over, grabbed his laptop from the nightstand, and logged onto the Internet. He typed *Swim SidewayZ* into the browser's search bar but received the message *No results found, did you mean: Swim Sideways?* Though he didn't discover why the dolphins pronounced the word with a Z, he clicked on the suggestion anyway. Eight links from the top, he found an article on water safety tips, positioned the cursor arrow on the title, and doubled clicked. The article listed a number of safety tips. One in particular fully awakened him. ***If caught in a rip current, swim sideways until free, don't swim against the current's pull.*** "This was why the dolphins had encouraged me to Swim Sideways," Ed said to himself. He had not imagined the dolphins after all, not when he was floating on his back in the ocean, nor when the dolphins had called out to him as he collected himself on the beach.

Now, assured that he was in his right mind, Ed searched for more information on surviving in a rip tide. He learned that rip tides, or "rip currents," are long, narrow bands of water that quickly pull any object, including people, away from the shore and out to sea. Reading on, he also learned that rip tides are dangerous but relatively easy to escape from if the individual remains calm. Then he read a passage that sent cold chills down his spine. *Do not struggle against the current. Rip tide deaths are not caused by the tides themselves; people become exhausted struggling against the current and cannot make it back to shore. Do not fight against the current, you will lose. Swim parallel to shore, across the current. A riptide is less than 100 feet wide, so swimming beyond it should not be too difficult.*

Ed sat there staring at the words on the computer screen, reflecting on his ordeal and realizing that, given the knowledge he had just acquired, he could have easily navigated his way out of trouble.

Reading the article reminded Ed how close he had come to losing his life and triggered the anxiety he felt during the drive home from the beach. To calm himself, he reflected on two salient principles from the ordeal: we rely on the service of others, and sometimes other life forms, for our mere existence; and we should remain open to the possibility that anything can, and will happen, even that dolphins can speak English and possess the altruism to rescue us from the sea.

Ed now craved for more information about dolphins. "What is the life of a dolphin?" was the question that preoccupied his thoughts, so he followed his mind and entered the question into the search window of his browser. The first article he came across discussed the life of a Bottlenose dolphin named "Jojo." The article supported the claim about dolphins made in the newspaper article Anne had retrieved from her journal. They had a penchant for rescuing people from shark attacks. As the article went, "Jojo" was a lone dolphin whose bond to one human was so strong that the creature remembered him after a four-month absence, and even saved him from a shark attack."

Ed was astonished not just by the confirmation that dolphins possessed the trait of altruism, but because they also could identify people whom they had met in the past. For him, this meant that they were certainly social creatures for whom relationships were essential, so essential that they were willing to risk their lives to protect those with whom they felt a bond. He wondered if the dolphins that saved him would remember him if he ever had the good fortune to encounter them again. He so much wanted to see them again; he wanted to thank them, though he wasn't sure how one expressed thanks to a dolphin.

He held onto that thought as he continued to read the article and discovered a characteristic of dolphins that further explained the behavior of his dolphin rescuers.

"A group of dolphins demonstrated some impressive strategic planning and teamwork as they feed on a school of fish, herding their prey and waiting for their turns so that everyone can get more food." "Wow," Ed thought. "Dolphins are strategic thinkers who use teamwork and sharing as values for group governance, maximizing their efficiency as hunters and distributing resources to nourish all members of their pods.

Another article spoke of the dolphin's family values. Dolphins are cooperative and help others in the pod. "Nannies" or "aunts" will watch over the calves of others while mothers are feeding. Clearly, Ed thought to himself, they are a species that understands the value of interdependence, something that he could benefit from. Especially impressive to Ed was the notion that mothers would trust the safekeeping of their calves to others. The demonstration of this level of trust, along with the other values, made an impression on Ed, but the trust behavior, unlike the others, caused a visceral reaction in Ed that he couldn't explain.

Ed's eyelids began to grow heavy. He could feel a blanket of exhaustion descending upon him. The weight of the anxiety that he had not been able to jettison was now lifting as he fell off to sleep. As he did, his hand slipped off the toggle button and startled him awake. When he returned to the screen to shut down the computer, he discovered the cursor resting on an article that would allay a lingering thought he had, which in spite of all he had read about dolphins, kept him from fully accepting the idea that Bottlenose dolphins rescued him from the sea. "Can dolphins speak English?" The article didn't answer his question fully, but it came close. As the article went, scientists studying the vocalizations and dialects of dolphins living in the waters off the western coast of Ireland discussed their analysis of 1,882 whistles from dolphins; astonishingly, they found 32 different categories of sounds and concluded the information had to be different given the diversity of areas where the dolphins resided.

If the scientists were correct, then the environments in which they resided, much like the dialects of people, influenced dolphin vocalizations. Ed thought, "Could it be that the dolphins that saved me had taken this trait to another level and also learned to speak human languages?" While he understood that he had no way to prove it, he was now open to the possibility. Moreover, Ed took away from this article something else: dolphins were adaptable creatures, in touch with their environment in ways that supported their need to build a strong bond with other dolphins, no matter where they encountered them. Then he paused and said to himself, "and people too."

Ed logged off the Internet, shut down the computer, and placed the laptop back on the nightstand. He rolled over, hugged Anne, kissed her on the back of her neck, and snuggled up for a good night's sleep.

As he began to doze off he could hear Anne whisper out of a deep sleep, "Swim SidewayZ Ed, Swim SidewayZ." Ed smiled and whispered back, "I love you, Honey," and then drifted into a dream that would change his life and Prescott, Inc. forever.

He found himself back in the ocean trying to swim to shore but stuck in a rip tide. As he began to struggle, the dolphins reappeared and encouraged him to "Swim SidewayZ." At first he repeated his mistake of swimming into the current. Then the dolphins repeated their instructions. Recognizing the instructions, he heeded their advice. He turned himself parallel to the shore and began to swim sideways and with every stroke, he felt his body knifing forward through the strong current. He felt elated that he had discovered a way to conquer the power of the currents, and the confidence to save his own life.

He could hear the dolphins cheering for him. "Way to go Ed, Swim SidewayZ out of danger, Swim SidewayZ out of bad habits, Swim SidewayZ to get ahead."

Soon Ed was clear of the current and succeeded in swimming to shore. When he was clear of the waves, he stood up and looked back to see the dolphins skipping backwards on their fluke fins. He yelled out to them, "Thank you, my friends, thank you for teaching me to Swim SidewayZ. I know that I'm dreaming, but I know you're real."

Then the dolphins yelled back, "It doesn't matter that you are asleep, what matters is that you have learned to Swim SidewayZ, and that we're real. Now, take what you have learned and Swim SidewayZ in other areas of your life!" With that, they dove into the ocean and disappeared. Realizing he had not learned the significance of Z in the word, Ed cried out feebly, "But why the letter Z?"

To his surprise, the dolphins broke from the sea and called back, "The shape of the letter Z is to remind you to Swim SidewayZ through the strong currents of life and business and to encourage others to do the same. The top and bottom lines of the letter represent swimming across the current and the diagonal line signifies there is seldom a direct route to the solutions of complex problems."

Ed walked out of the water and stood on the beach. He thought, "What all have I learned tonight and to what shall I apply this lesson?" First he thought, "Did the dolphins mean the lesson they had taught him? Well, of course that's what they meant." Then he had a startling revelation, maybe that's not what they meant at all. He remembered that they had said: It didn't matter that I was asleep. He thought, "Whoa, how did they know I was asleep and speaking to them in my dream?" Ed began to feel anxious, so he calmed himself by repeating the words "Swim SidewayZ." He was encouraging himself to accept the possibility that he had accessed a "dream reality," where the dolphins could connect with him in his dreams.

While it seemed far-fetched, Ed figured that if he was willing to accept the possibility that dolphins could speak English, he should be open to the idea that they have the power to reach him in his dreams. This thought calmed his anxiety and led him to the notion that the dolphins were probably referring to more than the lessons they taught him, but also, the principles he learned from surfing the Net about dolphin life. It dawned on him how ironically "surfing" and "net" were things that came to mind in the context of the dolphins. One word gave him a feeling of delight as he envisioned the dolphins riding and effortlessly playing on huge, mountainous waves, while the other word caused him fear and disgust as he pictured dolphins drowned in the nets of anglers, or trapped, trained, and used as entertainment in marine parks. He vowed to commit himself to the protection of dolphins. For the remainder of his life, Ed would donate his time and portions of all his earnings to the different foundations that worked to protect dolphins from anglers and exploitation.

"So, what have I learned?" Ed whispered to himself as he picked up a piece of driftwood and began to write in the sand. What came to mind first was what he had learned from the dolphins about how to survive a rip tide, so he wrote:

Swim SidewayZ ...

Out of danger

To change bad habits

To get ahead

Indeed, Swimming SidewayZ had taught him how to manage a dangerous situation successfully, but it also taught him how to respond in a crisis. He had tried to solve his problems through sheer determination and didn't employ his power of thinking clearly amidst chaos. He also found that he could get ahead by making a simple adjustment and by remaining calm. He was extremely grateful for a second chance to learn. Ed remembered how vulnerable the experience had made him feel and how dependent he was on the dolphins. He felt fortunate to be given a second chance to get things right.

Ed reflected on all he had learned about dolphin behavior from surfing the Internet. He recalled how "Jojo" the dolphin had bonded with a diver from its past, and saved him from a shark attack. Ed was astonished that dolphins would risk their lives for life forms other than their own. For some reason, he thought of marine mammals as being less intelligent and social than those on land. It became clear to him: dolphins were values centric creatures. Inspired by the revelation, he scooted over, brushed a pile of seaweed away, and wrote two separate messages about what he had learned about and from the Dolphin Values.

- In one way or another, everything in the world is connected.
- Everything is dependent on something else for its existence, survival, and success.
- Everyone desires a second chance to get things right.

Ed awoke from his dream feeling energized, courageous, and more importantly, more understanding of what to do to start leading Preston, Inc. through the rough currents the economic downturn was causing in its industry. He was eager and excited to tell Anne all about what he had learned during the dream.

Turning over and discovering Anne had already gotten up, Ed hopped out of bed and dashed into the bathroom, but didn't find her there. He then rushed into the kitchen and found her at the counter preparing lunch.

"Good morning sleepy head, it's about time you got up. I tried to wake you a couple of times; I couldn't stir you with a push or a kiss. I almost tried the mirror test, but I saw your hands moving as if you were writing something."

"You saw my hands moving as if I were writing something?" Ed asked, intrigued.

"Yes, Hon, you were writing on the bed as if you were writing on a large sheet of paper the letter 'Z.' I said to myself, 'Oh, he must be having a dream.' I only grew a little concerned because you slept straight through breakfast. It's now 11:30 a.m. What time did you fall asleep?" Anne asked as she tossed the salad.

Ed paused for a moment, and said reflectively, "I don't know, but it wasn't so late that I should have slept through breakfast," he replied. Then inquisitively he said, "I must have been some kind of tired to sleep for that many hours, but I did have a most unusual dream."

Bringing their lunch to the table, Anne asked, "Is that what you wanted to talk to me about when you rushed in here, Hon? I haven't seen you that excited in a long time."

"Yes," replied Ed. Then he told Anne everything he experienced during the dream. He wrote the affirmations and values he had scribbled into the sand onto a couple of paper napkins to show to Anne.

The Importance of the Letter "Z"
Remember to Swim SidewayZ out of the strong currents of life and business and teach others to do the same.

Dolphin Values
An unselfish concern for others

Strategic thinking

Teamwork

Inclusion

Maximize efficiency

As he showed the list to Anne, she could see that Ed had tears in his eyes.

"What's the matter dear?" she inquired.

Ed put his hand on top of hers and said softly, "I feel so fortunate to have received a second chance to learn from my mistakes. The dolphins reconnecting with me in my dream and telling me to take what I learned and apply it to my life seems like a good omen. I feel as though I received the ideal framework for navigating my business through the tough times we're facing." Then he paused to assess Anne's view on all that he said. Anne wiped the tears from Ed's face and stirred past the well of tears damned against his eyelids. She told him that she was grateful, too, for a second chance to love him even more.

Ed took Anne into his arms, hugged her tightly, and told her that he was thankful that she was in his life. He thanked her for loving him unconditionally and for always knowing what to say and do to help him manage his self-doubt, and the anxieties caused by the business.

Imbued with the certainty of Anne's unconditional faith and love for him, Ed reflected on something he had forgotten to tell Anne about his dream. He recalled the overwhelming visceral reaction he had had to the profound expression of trust the dolphin mothers demonstrated in letting other females baby-sit their babies. He told Anne that he was confused about why he had such a strong emotional reaction to this particular behavior of the dolphins. Anxious to get a better understanding of why he felt this way, he asked Anne if she felt that he trusted her.

Anne responded without the slightest hesitation, "Ed, of course I do, Honey. I know you trust me, and I never doubted that." As only a person who knew someone as well as Anne had come to know Ed, being together for over thirty years, Anne foresaw Ed's next question. She interjected before he could ask it, "But I'm not so sure your management team at Preston feels the same way, Hon …"

Ed's face dropped, not because of his predictability with Anne, but because he knew she was right. Moreover, he realized that the strong, visceral reaction he had had to the display of trust among the dolphins was the welling up of the cumulative self-denials about the price he would ultimately have to pay for not including his management team in decision-making.

After letting out a huge sigh, Ed kissed Anne on the cheek and said, "Baby, you're always on target; I appreciate your candidness and courage. I know how hard it must have been to say that to me, and I know, while you haven't said it in exactly that way, you have tried to let me know this before, I just didn't' want to hear it. I guess I've got too much of Hans Sorenson and my dad stored up in me." Then Ed smiled, and said, "I got a lot of work to do come Monday morning."

"That's right. Now you know just what to do, Hon," Anne said, and then offered more huzzahs. "Do the things you learned in your dream, then trust your team; they want to prove to you that they're trustworthy. Besides, the dolphins emphasized the importance of the 'Z.' Didn't they to teach others to do the same?" Anne's encouragement fueled Ed's enthusiasm and his confidence in what he had learned from the dolphins during his dream.

Ed began to explain the strategy he was going to present to his team on Monday.

Anne politely interrupted, "Now Hon, you asked me if I felt trusted by you."

"Yes, I did," Ed said as he prepared to explain his strategy, but again Anne interrupted him.

Pressing her fingers gently against his pursed lips, she whispered, "Then trust me and eat your lunch; I want to use the remainder of the weekend to take advantage of the blessing of having had your life spared, my love."

Ed reflected on those tender words, smiled effusively, took Anne's fingers that were still resting on his lips, and gentled kiss each one of them. He then took in a hearty fork full of a salad consisting of fresh organic Arugula, sweet and spicy pecans, cherry tomatoes, avocado, and warm goat's cheese.

Chapter 3

Ed was in the offices of Preston Incorporated on Monday morning before anyone else. He was in the conference room reviewing the notes he had prepared the night before to present to his executive management team. He couldn't remember the last time he felt so nervous and excited about having a meeting. The closest he came was in 1992 when he announced to the company that they had reached the $10 million dollar mark in net revenue.

On this morning he intended to share with the group the concepts and values he had acquired during the dream when he had had a second opportunity to learn from the dolphins. He had not decided to discuss the pivotal dream experience itself, nor the harrowing first encounter with the rip currents, nor the surreal and fantastical encounter he had had with the dolphins. He thought that being transparent about all that had happened and all that he had learned would suffice as demonstrating that he trusted his team. Ed figured that if he could strengthen the trust between himself and his managers, he could turn things around at Preston. Maybe by heightening the trust quotient he could stimulate the team's productivity in some way.

Ed meticulously wrote all the notes he had prepared onto flip-chart paper and positioned them on the conference table. The notes included a moniker that rested closest to his heart: the dolphin values, about being open to the possibility of miracles, and the importance of the letter Z.

As Ed finished posting one of the charts on the wall, his VPs began filing into the room.

"Mornin' Ed," one team member said.

"Good morrrrrning!!" another one called out.

"My, my, aren't we focused this morning. Has someone had a slight brainstorm over the weekend," a team member said as they filed into the room.

"Good morning, folks," Ed said, as he took a sip of coffee.

As everyone took a seat, Ed opened the meeting by mentioning that he had called the meeting to share some thoughts about injecting a stronger spirit of togetherness into the organization. He mentioned he knew that many people in the room didn't feel as though he trusted their ideas and suggestions, and that, for the most part, he had been the cause of that.

Going further, he mentioned that it was his desire to try to change that aspect of his relationship with them. He stressed that if there was ever a time when their input was needed it was now, what with the company facing unprecedented losses due to the national recession and the subsequent downturn in their industry. With that, Ed turned toward the wall and read from the first chart.

Ed had a visceral reaction again as he read the words from the flip chart. As goose bumps covered his body he expounded on the meaning of his newfound philosophy. "I will be working to make some changes to my approach to leadership; to this point in our relationship, I thought it was my responsibility to have all the answers and that your duty was to carry out my orders. I can't believe I've been that stupid all these years. I'm sorry that it has taken so long for me to realize this. I apologize if I made any of you feel subject."

In one way or another, everything in the world is connected; everything is dependent on something else for its existence, survival, and success.

Everyone desires a second chance to get things right.

Through moistened eyes, Ed panned the room and asked, "Are there any questions?"

Brenda, the VP of Human Resources, spoke up first. "Ed, I'm not comfortable with you calling yourself stupid. That language is a bit harsh; I don't remember any of us complaining that you were making all the decisions. If you ask me, I think we're all a little guilty of complacency."

"That's fine and all Brenda, but I need to know that I wasn't leading as though I was truly connected to you guys. I never took into consideration that maybe people need to be a part of making decisions that influence the direction the company was going in, in how their lives would be affected."

"I agree with Ed, Brenda," Jim, the VP of finance and accounting, chimed.

"Is that so?" Carl, the VP of production, interjected.

"What do you mean?" retorted Jim.

"Certainly, you don't think Ed meant to exclude us from participating in shaping the direction of the company?" Carl asked acerbically.

"Well, no I don't believe that it was his intention, but I think it served his need for control. His need for control was greater than his desire to include us in strategic planning or decision making. I think it was easy for Ed and the rest of us to get complacent, given the phenomenal success the company has had since Ed took over ownership. We have never had as much as a bad quarter in all that time," stated Brenda emphatically.

Looking around the room for a reaction, with none offered, she continued. "I can't speak for Jim, but I think I understand where he's coming from. At times I felt frustration when it seemed that Ed needed to do a better job with HR in strategic planning for the company.

However, I could have done a better job being an advocate of my ideas and those submitted by my team. Yes, I know what all the textbooks on leadership say about leaders setting the climate and being a model and steward of organizational culture, but we're not children here. We are all intelligent adults. If, at some point, we felt that Ed wasn't living up to our expectations or giving tepid support to our ideas, we had a duty to speak up."

Taken aback by Brenda's comments, Jim fired back, "Give me a break, why don't you," offering a sarcastic chuckle to hide his argumentative temperament.

Ed looked at Jim quizzically and silently searched for a past incident between them that may have left him bitter. His reflection revealed nothing of significance.

"Is that tone really necessary?" asked Bennington, the VP of sales and marketing, "I mean, really, Jim!" Oh, I see. I'm the only one here that feels frustrated with the way Ed has been running things around here. I mean, I can appreciate Brenda's point about us not being assertive and all, but Ed has not exactly made it easy for us to feel safe in speaking our minds at meetings. The Ed I'm listening to this morning is a drastically different person than the one I've been reporting to for the last ten years."

Ed, sensing both anger and, more importantly, a heavy sense of dissatisfaction in Jim's words, said, "It seems that I wasn't listening to you Jim, and I'm sorry for that. What can I do to help us move forward in our relationship?"

Jim paused with shock. In the past, Ed, while never overtly disrespectful toward him, had made him feel marginalized by his prosaic nature, which grew acute whenever he was under stress or confronted with situations full of uncertainty.

Sounding more tempered, Jim continued, "Well, for one, you can show more interest in my ideas and concerns; I mean, a lot of what we're wrestling with involves reduced revenue, which is in large part due to the saturation in our market by the arrival of new competition. Bennington will never say it, but his presentation five years ago on economic trends, in particular, the emergence of interest-only loans and aberrant increases in property values, were prescient given the environment we find ourselves in today."

As Ed turned to make eye contact with Bennington, he was met with a supportive smile.

"Jim's right, and so is Brenda," Bennington said in his usual monotone, emotionless manner. "I'm not an I-told-you-so kind of person, and I'm not implying that that is what Jim was intimating. I would have appreciated if you could have given more attention to what was forecasted in my presentation. Moreover, I was perplexed that you didn't inquire more about the strategy portion of the presentation, about generating additional streams of income. I think my strategy to diversify into areas where our skills and knowledge were transferable and supportable by our resources at the time may have produced some favorable results given the talent in this room."

There had been nothing said by the team that was inaccurate or spiteful, it was all true. He hadn't heard these things before, but now they resonated in his soul. It was the most transparent any of his VPs had ever been with him and it was the most vulnerable he had ever been with them.

He was hurting. He was nonconfrontational by nature and interpersonal conflict, or critical feedback about his performance, or that of the company, depleted him of his creative energy and confidence. He knew it was an inherited trait from his dad, but until now, it had not been a challenge to the changes he needed to make in himself and his leadership and management style. He knew that he had not established a climate of trust with his team, but he had no idea it had affected them to this degree. He also discovered another consequence of his autocratic leadership style: not only had he missed an opportunity to leverage the human talent among his executive team, but he had also missed an opportunity over the years to develop himself and the people who counted on him for direction.

As Ed reflected on all of what was happening to him and in him, Carl pierced his veil of introspection: "Ed, though it's taken years for us to get to this point, what is going on with the business that caused this shift in your approach?" he asked quizzically. Before Ed could respond, Carl continued, "or should I ask this question of others in the room," Carl said, looking around the room inquisitively, only to see expressions and gestures meant to deescalate the tension.

Ed could feel an anxiety in him and after taking a nanosecond to review the possibilities, attributed it to his reluctance to speak about the very impetuous behind his change in behavior, and his experience with the dolphins. Feeling ambivalence and confusion mounting, he blurted, "Hey," then looking at his watch proffered, "we've been at it for two hours, anybody need a break?" They approved. "Take ten," Ed declared with exasperation.

With the team dispersed, Ed eased into his chair and discovered that he had perspired profusely underneath his clothes, even saturating his underwear. Unnerved by his strange tension, Ed called Anne on her cell phone:

"Hey, Hon!" Anne exclaimed with great excitement. "Having fun yet?" she asked confidently.

"Well, yes and no. I mean, what I mean is, that, um, well, darn, I just don't feel very confident being this open with the team."

"Did something happen Ed, I mean; is there something wrong, Hon?"

"No, there are a lot of good things going on here," Ed assured her. "These folks are telling me things about my leadership behavior that I should have had known about years ago."

"Oh, good, then you must have told them about the dream! Hon, I knew that would get people buzzing!" Anne said, not fully understanding his message.

Ed allowed Anne's words to sink in for a minute. They rang true not because they would have produced the effect she described, but because they exposed the reason for the tension he felt. He was afraid to tell the story of the dolphins; as a result, he was being disingenuous with himself and about the value of teamwork he admired in the dolphins. He said to Anne, "How can I even begin to practice team work if I can't trust my team enough to share such a life-changing event with them, especially one that prompted my actions."

Anne, with agreement in her voice, said, "Hon, don't worry about it; trust yourself, and in the possibility of miracles, have you shared that principle with the team?" She exclaimed gleefully, "That's the one I love the most. I think about what that means to me in my own life, and don't forget about the importance of the Z!"

"Okay, dear, I'll tell them, I mean, I owe it to them, and myself, to put that story into action. If it can have such a powerful impact on you then it should have the same effect on anyone who hears it," Ed said with growing confidence.

"That's the spirit, Hon! Have fun with it Babe, just go with the flow, just Swim SidewayZ!" Anne said sanguinely.

"Thanks good lookin,'" Ed said, and gave Anne a loving peck through the phone.

"Thanks for getting back on time!" Ed exclaimed as the team entered the room, still chatting from their break. He proceeded over the banter as the team milled around the refreshments at the back of the room. "It would be disingenuous of me if I went any further with our discussion without telling you what happened to me over the weekend. Carl's inquiry about the impetuous of this meeting deserves an honest answer." Ed's pronouncement broke the chatter as people slowly returned to their seats.

For the next fifteen minutes, Ed told the story of his near drowning and rescue by the dolphins and the reflective dream he experienced after the incident. No detail was unaccounted, including the Internet searches he made and the newspaper article Anne retrieved from her desk about the propensity of dolphins to bond with humans. He mentioned that the message on the flip chart had come from the experience, as did those on the table. "I was afraid to tell you of this for fear you would think I had cracked under the stress of all we're going through as a company," Ed said pensively.

"Wow, what a fantastic story!" Please tell me that you're not making it all up; I've heard and read stories about the altruism of dolphins, but I must admit, I received them through the same inspective filter I use for stories about UFOs. It's not that I don't believe in UFOs, but some of those stories are hard to believe," Jim said nonchalantly.

"I've never been more sincere in my life, Jim," Ed assured him.

"Bennington, are you alright?" Brenda asked. His attention was drawn to her question to Bennington. Confirming her suspicions, he was suffering great consternation. Tears streamed down his cheeks and he wrung his hands.

Through muddled tones he replied, "Yes. I'm fine, but I feel great ambivalence. On the one hand, I feel so relieved that Ed's life was spared. To think that we could have been in this room this morning grieving and trying to figure out a succession strategy is a sad thought. On the other hand, I feel distraught that Ed was even thinking that we wouldn't believe him."

"Those were my thoughts exactly. I was sitting here trying to figure out what messages I may have sent to Ed that would have made him feel as though I wouldn't support him in a moment such as this," said Brenda.

As Ed paused to think of a response to Brenda's statement, Jim, to everyone's astonishment, rose from his chair and traversed the room to where Ed stood and embraced him in a big bear hug. Slowly, each member of the team joined in and took turns giving Ed hugs of such vivacity that he felt completely assured of their belief in him.

When they had finished hugging Ed, he was awash in acceptance and assurance. "There isn't a thing that you folks did or said that caused me to doubt whether you would believe my story; my hesitation is a product of my own self-doubt and penchant to think the worst where you are concerned. I will never subject you or myself to this again, I promise." Then he pointed back to the flip chart as he read his statement about connectivity and deserving second chances, while adding a phrase about the importance of trust:

"We are all connected and interdependent and deserve a chance to get things right. Our connections are stronger when we learn to trust one another enough to be transparent with our feelings, ideas, opinions, and facts of mutual importance."

Inspired, Brenda offered a suggestion. "Hey, I have an idea. What if we used this statement as a daily affirmation and posted it on the walls in our offices and throughout the company? If it can have this effect on us then why should it not have the same effect on the rest of the company?" Brenda asked enthusiastically.

"Sure, it makes sense to me," said Jim.

"Yeah, sounds like a very smart strategy," said Bennington.

"I'm on board," shouted Carl.

"What say you there, Ed?" Jim queried.

Striking a pensive pose, Ed, in his usual monotone manner, uttered, "Let's do it."

This prompted Jim to chide, "That's something else we need to work on."

"And what might that be?" said Ed.

"Putting more inflection into your speaking style." With that, everyone broke out in laughter. Then Brenda said, "That is probably more important than you think, Ed."

"Say more," encouraged Ed.

"Well, I think giving more variety to your spoken words is important for accurately representing your feelings and ideas," offered Brenda.

"Okay, thanks Brenda for saying that," said Carl, "it gives me a great idea. Think about it, what besides the affirmation, caused us to open up today?"

The team pondered the question. "The financial state of the company?" asked Brenda.

"Well, not quite," said Carl.

"You're right," interjected Brenda with joy.

"Wow, we have been operating under the mantle of transparency," said Carl. "Though painful at times, it has facilitated a sharing of information between us that has led us to a greater understanding of our relationship with Ed, and given us a deeper understanding of ourselves and the role we may have played in creating our organization and the situation, we find ourselves in today."

"I concur," said Ed. "I know I'm different and better for having had this conversation with you all, and since we're talking about leadership, I will say that it's my duty to create more opportunities, opportunities for us to grow and develop, and be more transparent, forthcoming, and inclusive of you all in strategic planning and decision making."

"I'm glad you feel that way," said Carl, "because I think you should call an all-company meeting and tell everyone your story about the dolphins."

"Brilliant!" declared Bennington. "It would give you a chance to practice being more inflective in your speech and it will give us a great platform to introduce the company to the rationale behind the affirmation."

"Okay, Ben!" said Ed. "This time I won't ignore your suggestion. Give me a couple of weeks to work on my delivery and maybe get some help from Brenda, and I will call the company together and tell them my story."

Looking at the clock on the wall, Brenda sighed loudly and uttered, "I'm late for my 11:30 a.m. meeting with my managers. There seems to be a reoccurring conflict over sharing resources. There is a 'they're mine' attitude emerging which I think has something to do with the purchase restrictions I placed on managers. Now they are required to share certain tools and backroom staff."

"I see." said Ed, "Well, I was going to get into a discussion that I think will help you manage that situation and strengthen our culture and business practices in general. However, I understand that we can't get everything done today. What if we get back together again tomorrow morning so I can introduce you to some of my other ideas?"

"Does it have to do with Swimming SidewayZ?" asked Jim, wishfully. "I wanted to know if you had any plans to get more into that as a concept for how we might get out of this mess." Ed couldn't have asked for more.

"It has everything to do with that Carl; thanks for your support and enthusiasm. So, are we up for meeting again tomorrow?"

In unison, they all gave a shout of confirmation, collected their belongings, and exited the room.

As Ed put things in order for their meeting the next morning, he looked up to see that Jim had doubled back to write a message on the flip chart.

The two men looked each other in the eye and smiled.

It is never too late to say
you are sorry.

Everyone deserves a second chance
to get things right.

Chapter 4

Early Tuesday morning Ed walked into the office of Preston, Inc. and made a beeline for the conference room to begin his second session with the team. He was more excited than he had been the day before. To his surprise, he wasn't the first to arrive; waiting for him with their coffees and bagels was the entire executive management team. "Goood morning, Ed," they said in unison.

Further energized by their obvious enthusiasm Ed said, "Alright, let's get started," and proceeded to post one of the messages on the wall.

Dolphin Values

An unselfish concern for others
Strategic Thinking
Teamwork
Inclusion
Maximum Efficiency

Continuing with the discussion from Monday about his research on dolphins, Ed said, "One other thing, I came away with from my research on the dolphins is the way they appear to function using a set of values.

As I thought about the marvelous ways the dolphins lived their lives, I began categorizing their behaviors in terms of core values. The more I thought about it the more I wondered what the effect their values would have on our organization. After all, if dolphins can function according to a set of acceptable behaviors, why can't we?" Ed asked.

Brenda immediately offered her view. "Ed, are you saying that you believe we don't function by a set of values or principles?"

"Well, I---yeah, I guess I'm, Brenda. Everything I know about organizations and human groups tells me that it would be virtually impossible for groups, and/or individuals to function without them. Here's what I'm trying to say; values are something people use to manage their behavior and make certain choices. Without them, people won't have any conscience about anything that they do."

"Very interesting," said Brenda. "So what you are saying is similar to what an organizational development consultant taught the management group I was a part of at my last job."

"Say more," said Ed.

"I'm paraphrasing, but what he basically said was, 'values are always present, though often, individuals, groups, teams, families, and organizations function without a conscious understanding that they are operating according to a set of values.' In other words, they often exist implicitly."

"Very good then, we will operate more explicitly with our values," said Ed. What I had in mind was to have us take these values and use them to remind us what is important to us. I've ranked these values in accordance with their importance to the company. I want us to post these on the walls throughout the company, along with the affirmation. As we agreed, I would discuss where these values came from during my all-company meeting, the story about how the dolphins demonstrated these values should be a fine example that the values can work for us.

As Ed explained his strategy the room grew quiet, contrasting the enthusiasm that represented the meeting in the beginning. Sensing the atmosphere had changed, Ed paused to give space to the sudden stillness. After what seemed an hour, one of the group members pierced the deafening quiet.

"Let go so I can grow!" pleaded Bennington. I got a lot out of yesterday's meeting; it was the most personally transformative meeting I've had in the five years since I joined the company. Think about it Ed, you've got teamwork, inclusion, and sharing up there as values you were impressed to see the dolphins using, but you're not practicing them. You need to let go!"

It was a "wow" moment for Ed and the group because the statement was representative of the issue that had prompted their willingness to return for the

Tuesday meeting. Now they were re-experiencing the Ed they had known all along, the one who had to have complete control of the meeting, who was using the autocratic and exclusive style of management that had caused them to feel frustrated in the first place.

Sensing Ed was at a loss about how to regain the collaborative spirit of the meeting and to get unstuck from his primary style of management, Brenda acted officiously. "Hey Ed, are you open to suggestions about how to move forward with implementing the values?"

Recognizing that Brenda was encouraging him to Swim SidewayZ as a leader, Ed didn't make the mistake he had made the first time with the dolphins. "Absolutely," he exclaimed, "what did you have in mind."

"Well, I thought maybe I could contact the consultant that worked on values with us at my last job."

"Well, don't you think that depends on what he did for the company, and whether it was worth the investment?" asked Jim.

"That's a good point, Jim," said Carl. "No offense Ed, but our decision-making processes could benefit from a bit more wisdom." Now we're talking. As I've been saying for years, especially for issues of considerable uncertainty and complexity, our cycle is too short and lacks proven methodologies," chimed Jim.

"I agree. Ed, I've never had any problem with the simple decisions you have made for the company, but I have great angst with the difficult ones made without our input. For instance, what are some of the methodological approaches you're referring to Jim?" asked Bennington.

"Well, I'm no expert on the subject, but I've been reading a few books. In particular, one I read suggested that for situations of great uncertainty, scenario analysis and learning is a good approach. Others suggest fault tree analysis, and others pro/con, etc."

Ed received an earful. The team's eagerness to participate in decision making and problem solving fascinated him. He wanted to dive right into unpacking all that Jim had learned about decision-making methodologies, but his intuition told him that this wasn't the central theme of the meeting. Nevertheless, he perceived the lack of synergy at the company and admitted to himself that it was because he had not done a proper job of involving his management team in helping him lead the company. After all, he had enough sense to know they were his primary change agents. He knew that he had to let go if he, his team, and the organization could grow. And, he had to start by letting go of his need for control.

He wasn't sure why, but he believed the emergence of the dolphin's values-centric life solidified his opinion about what was the most crucial element the company needed for turning itself around. Therefore, having fostered a climate of collaboration and respect, he interjected, "Jim, would it be okay if I asked you to prepare an informative presentation on the decision-making methodologies that you have discovered and present it to us?"

"I can do that! When do you need me to have that ready?" asked Jim, grabbing his pen and making a note to himself.

"Let's get together in your office after the meeting to discuss it," said Ed.

"Sounds good to me," chirped Jim.

"What I would like to suggest is that we follow up on Brenda's suggestion to get in touch with the consultant and see if he is a fit for us," said Ed. "How many people think this would be a good idea?"

The whole room raised their hands and nodded their heads in agreement. "Great!"

"Okay, when do you want me to get in touch with him," asked Brenda.

Bennington immediately offered his opinion while looking in Ed's direction. "Why not right now? After all, we're stuck as to what to do with the values, are we not?" Ed nodded his head in agreement and suggested they take a ten-minute break while Brenda tried to contact the consultant.

"Super, I'll call him then," said Brenda.

As the team exited the room, Ed hung back to mull over all they had said. He was surprised that he struggled with the concept of introducing the values to the team. In fact, other than posting them on the wall, he had not had a chance to speak to what each one of them meant in the context of the organization because the team became so engrossed in discussions about processes.

The tension he was experiencing had to do with his practice of making decisions exclusive of others. It was troubling him that in his excitement about the Dolphin Values, he had not contemplated what to do with the values in order to make them operational. Though aware that this wasn't the root of his discontent, he was discovering he had a strong need for control, in particular, a need for decisions to be his own.

As he reflected back to the first encounter with the dolphins, he realized he had not responded to their instructions. Not simply because he thought they were a figment of his imagination, but because he was "hardwired" to do things his way. It was an attitude he had inherited from his father. Being in the rip tide, he was on a treadmill at sea, and still he was determined to solve the problem in his own way without the inclusion of the dolphins. His behavior was characteristic of the adage about doing the same thing over-and-over without getting a different result, but expecting one.

Shifting away from thoughts about his lack of proficiencies and to a mental frame involving collaboration with his team, Ed saw the real value of having introduced the team to the Dolphin Values. The values created a discussion on how to function like an organization and a team. He was already experiencing something powerful about values; they had an element of accountability associated with them. Ed was correct, but he had no idea how vital his introduction of the dolphin's values would be for the company.

The team, all except Brenda, had returned from the break. Ed welcomed them back and thanked them for retuning on time.

He was wrestling with the next steps to take with the values when Brenda rushed into the room. "Sorry for being a bit tardy folks, but I got some good news. I spoke with Trevor Bradshaw, the consultant you asked me to contact, and he is willing to stop by and answer any questions we have."

"You mean this morning?" asked Carl surprisingly.

"Yes, he said he can be here in thirty minutes and could spend an hour or two with us."

Ed paused for a moment then asked, "Well, what do you all think?"

"And, how much are those two hours going to cost us?" asked Jim.

"Zero," replied Brenda enthusiastically.

"You must be kidding!" said Carl, astonished. "In all my years in business, I've never encountered a consultant that didn't charge something. They either charge too much or charge you for too long!" he said cynically.

"Well, since I sense a bit of skepticism, I will tell you what he said. He said that since he was already in the area and because I remembered him and had such confidence in him that he would offer us his services gratis; if we wanted to proceed further he would work out an agreement based on the need and his availability. What shall I tell him? I told him I would call him back after I spoke with the team."

Ed surveyed the room for a decision and all the members of the team nodded their heads in the affirmative. Ed then asked the group if he could have a verbal response for the record.

They all said, "Let go so we can grow!" Ed lit up a big smile and said, "Okay, Brenda, give the man a call."

Within thirty minutes, Trevor Bradshaw was standing in front of the team introducing himself and passing out his business cards. Trevor was in his early forties and still maintained the athletic physique he depended on during his youth. He told the team that he launched Bradshaw Consulting and Training twenty  years ago after his retirement from a 15-year professional tennis career.

He mentioned that he had attended boarding school and Ivy League colleges for his undergraduate, graduate, and post-graduate work, all in organizational psychology.

He discussed that he had launched his consulting career in an attempt to fill the transitional career needs for tennis players. He explained that often many of them meandered through life after tennis trying to find a career, or worse, a way to lessen the disengagement trauma, which comes from detaching one's self from sports after being engrossed in it, in some cases since childhood.

More to the point, he spoke about core values orientation as a key factor in his success with assisting athletes. He discussed a strategy of teaching athletes the meaning and value of knowing their core values and needs as the motivational focal points behind their thoughts and actions, and consequently, the formulation of their interests and passions. He then explained that when he was successful with helping them develop an inventory of their current needs and core values, it facilitated their ability to think about their interests and passions. In other words, Trevor's experiences with athletes taught him that there was an interdependent relationship between needs, values, and helping athletes to identify their interests and passions, and eventually a method of self-governance and self-reliance.

He went on telling the team that he had found his way to the larger world of organizational consulting, training, and coaching when one of his first business clients used his coaching to ready himself for taking over his parent's string of car washes. It was during that assignment that he first discovered that the work he had done with individuals could expand to include interventions for an entire organization. He explained to the group that, like an individual, in order for an organization to achieve its mission and goals, they have to know and live out their values.

When he finished introducing himself and his theories to the team, Trevor asked them a question. "Brenda mentioned that you were experiencing some 'confusion' with implementing your values. Is that correct?"

"Well, they are not exactly our values. Is there a problem? I mean, is it okay to borrow values from others?" asked Ed.

"Sure, it's customary to borrow values; it's also not unprecedented to mimic the standards and procedures of other companies," Trevor replied confidently.

"Does that rule apply to Dolphin Values?" asked Jim with sanguine speculation, to the laughter of the team.

At a loss as to what Jim might be alluding to, but aware that he was on the receiving end of an inside joke, Trevor responded sheepishly, "Did you say Dolphin Values?"

"Let me explain," said Ed, and he recounted to Trevor what had taken place with him and the dolphins, including the dream.

"I would be lying to you if I told you all that I've heard that one before." Then, looking at Ed, he asked, after the laughter had died down a bit. "Did that really happen to you?" expecting Ed to relieve his suspicions that maybe he was putting him on.

Brenda responded, "Yes, it's a true story."

Trevor stood there in disbelief. Noticing his skepticism, Ed urged Trevor to let go so he could grow!

"What a fantastic story!" Trevor had decided to go with the flow. He thought maybe there was something to gain from this experience; after all, the whole team couldn't be insane ... he hoped. Then he joined in the laughter of the team, "Well, I will go with the flow because you said they were Bottlenose Dolphins. I've read that they were pretty smart mammals."

Then Trevor explained to the team the universality of needs and values, irrespective of cultures, and included in that the social worlds of Bottlenose Dolphins. What distinguishes us according to needs and values is the degree to which we fulfill them; in the case of values, it depends on what beliefs and behaviors we employ to demonstrate them.

"So let me see if I follow this," said Ed. "Are you saying that we can use the values identified as Dolphin Values and apply definitions and behaviors to them that reflect our culture?"

"Why sure you can, Ed," said Trevor. "Just make sure that you get input from as many of the people in the organization as you can."

Trevor's advice prompted Jim to offer an opinion. "Well, while I respect your experience at consulting on these matters, I think that the people at Preston would prefer management to make those kinds of decisions for them. Don't you think, guys? I mean, that's what we were paid to do, make management decisions."

"Well, there are those management theorists and consultants who would agree with you, but it has been my experience that that approach isn't a wise one. People want to have input in developing principles and behaviors that they'll be responsible to apply. After all, including people in the process would be taking the first step in practicing the intrinsic characteristic of the dolphin's teamwork and inclusion values. At the end of the day, it's your choice."

"That makes a lot of sense to me," Ben agreed. "Plus, by not opening up the process to the whole organization, we would, in effect, be guilty of doing what we accused Ed of doing to us, excluding us from participating in managing the company."

"Ok, you got a point there, Ben," said Jim. "I just feel that we're paid to make the important decisions and it seems to me that it's unfair to ask staff to assist in a task for which they are not being paid."

"I get your point Jim, and it's a good one," said Trevor. "Still, let me inform you all of something before I leave. The reason you would want to introduce values in an explicit way is so you can advance beyond the attitude that we're all merely duty bound. Values call us to embrace responsibility as a collective value. Through the values we're encouraged to do more than what our duties ask of us. We are provoked to seek additional ways to add value to our organizations, value that ultimately should be measurable in the form of a stronger climate, brand value, customer satisfaction, job security, profit margins, and a host of other beneficial outcomes that an organization's stakeholders will share."

Chapter 5

As the meeting adjourned, Brenda gave Trevor a hug and thanked him for taking the time out of his schedule to meet with the team, and told him how much she appreciated his input.

"The pleasure was all mine. It's not every day that I get an opportunity to work with a CEO whose leadership is influenced by talking dolphins," said Trevor.

"Yes, I guess it must be a first for you," said Brenda. "We all found Ed's experience quite fascinating, but if you know Ed, you know he isn't the type to make up stories. If he tells you something you can bet it's true and that he has given a lot of thought to it."

"Very interesting," said Trevor. "I will keep that in mind should I get to work with you on developing and operationalizing your values."

Ed, overhearing the conversation, took Trevor's hand, shook it, and expressed his gratitude to Trevor for coming in on such short notice. He then turned to Brenda, flashed a big smile, and thanked her for recommending Trevor to the group. "I can't thank you enough, Brenda, for referring Trevor to us. His insight and expertise were what we needed to move us forward."

"I'm glad I could help out," said Brenda.

"And I'm thankful and honored that I made such a good impression when we first met," said Trevor.

"Yep, something like that," said Brenda. "You were effective, and as I remember, you put us on the right track. After that we were able to develop a much stronger culture through your consulting and coaching."

"Thanks," said Trevor.

As the other team members passed by to thank Trevor, Ed excused himself and returned to his office to prepare for his meeting with their largest client. As he did, he thanked the team for their effort and their openness in discussing their ideas.

"No problem," said, Jim. "Thanks for giving us your trust."

The word trust stuck with Ed. No one on the team had ever expressed that to him before. He knew instinctively what he was hearing had to do with his conscious effort to be vulnerable in telling them the story about the dolphins. He had his honey, Anne, to thank for this.

Trevor made a mental note of Jim's statement, as well. His experience alerted him that there must be something significant about the emphasis Jim placed on the word trust.

As Ed looked over the new project proposal, he prepared for his largest client, Western Construction. His assistant called to let him know that Frank from Western had arrived and was waiting for him and the team in the conference room. Ed took a deep breath, slipped the proposal presentation underneath his arm, and headed for the conference room.

Western Construction had been a loyal customer for over 20 years. Representative of this bond was the fact that, for the past ten years, roughly 25% of Preston's gross annual revenue came from Western purchase orders. Ed and Western's CEO, Frank Broadus, had become good friends and assisted each other in making a lot of money for their respective companies. Nevertheless, the market downturn had significantly reduced the demand for new home construction and Western was beginning to experience the pain caused by lower demand for its custom homes. Thinking forward, Frank had perceived the market change coming and had expanded his customer base to include new and renovated hotel and motel construction, as well as local and state government building contracts. The purpose for his meeting with Ed and the team was to fill an order for 30,000 windows for a new government contract awarded to Western.

Unbeknownst to Ed, his competition, Just Frames, had approached Frank with a deal which would significantly lower Western's cost per unit, and Frank was giving serious thought to accepting the deal.

"Afternoon Frank, it's great to see you. How's the family?" Ed asked warmly.

"Marsha and the kids are well, thanks for asking," replied Frank.

"Please give them my best," said Ed.

"Will do," said Frank, "and the same to Ann."

"You betcha," said Ed.

Ed thanked Frank for allowing Preston an opportunity to present its proposal and proceeded to present Frank with the key features and benefits of his plan. Ed had done his homework and discovered that Just Frames was using a supplier who was going out of business, and, therefore, prepared to offer material far below market value in order to meet its financial obligations. Equipped with that information, he was able to compete with Just Frames on price and with that knowledge, he felt confident that his reputation for quality work and service would give him the edge. He needed to win Frank's business.

Assuming a confident posture, Ed asked if Frank had any questions. Frank replied that Ed and his team had made a terrific presentation and he was impressed with the lower cost per unit that Ed was able to offer him. With that, Ed extended an invitation to Frank to join him in developing a contract that would enable them to assist Western in meeting the needs of his client. At that moment Frank mentioned the additional offer he had received from Ed's competitor. Ed was thunderstruck by the revelation. Frank revealed that Just Frames had offered to make Western a 30% partner in its business, and a sum of cash, for rewarding them with the government contract. For a moment, neither he nor any of the members of the team knew what to say.

The news was staggering. Not only would it deprive Preston of the much-needed capital windfall, it would also signal the end of a business relationship that would most likely cause Preston to make some personnel cuts in the very near future, something Ed dreaded.

Ed stood there with a blank expression on his face. Just then, uncharacteristically, Bennington spoke up. Until Ed had launched the values' discussions, he often was reticent in meetings. "That is great news, Mr. Broadus. I'm not surprised you're thinking about entering into this partnership." The whole team directed their attention at Ben. Ed had no idea where Ben was going with his praise of Frank. Frank thanked him, but asked Ben why he thought so. "Well, I did the research which uncovered the information about the supplier who is going out of business, and upon discovery, I thought to myself, "Boy, Frank sure is serious about finding the best deals. I wondered to myself if you knew that the supplier was going out of business and wanted to see which of the bidders would make the same effort in order to find you the best deal."

Frank, shocked by Ben's assessment replied, "You are absolutely correct Ben. Thank you for being honest with me."

"Mr. Broadus, I think your strategy was a great one. No, actually, it was brilliant! With Ed's permission, I would like to ask a question."

With that, he looked to Ed for his support. Ed looked back in utter astonishment and gave Ben a nod, mixed with caution and desperation.

"Have you looked at the soft side of the deal with Just Frames? Thus far, both of our presentations have been all about the hard side, the bottom line stuff that determines all business decisions."

Frank replied that it was a good question and admitted that he had not in a strategic way. He asked Ben to be more specific.

"Well, as you probably know, a significant percentage of our gross annual revenue is attributed to doing business with Western."

"Yes, I did know that. If I'm not mistaken, Ed mentioned that it's a little over 20%."

"Yes, that's correct," said Ed. "While it's important for us always to be mindful of being thankful and vigilant in ensuring the performance of the practices that keep you a satisfied customer, the same holds true for you. I don't know what percentage of Just Frames business Western represents, but I venture to say that it probably doesn't match ours."

Frank leaned back in his chair and took a long, deep breath. He was starting to sense where Ben was going with his thinking.

"I think I get it," said Frank. "You're asking me why I would want to go into business with a company that received less of my business."

"Yes, this is my point," said Ben. "I'm also asking if you have considered why you have done so.

Clearly, we have always out-performed them. Can I ask, other than the 30%, what is your interest in Just Frames?"

"Well, yes," said Frank, "truth be told, they just put this deal together with their proposal. I haven't had a chance to evaluate the situation fully, or my interest, but I'm interested given the strength of their brand."

"Well, I would ask you to take a careful look at how their values align with their work and culture at Western. We, here at Preston, are in the process of being strategic in understanding how we can make values an asset in how we function as a company. Ed can tell you more about it, and if you were evaluating your deal with Just Frames, I would strongly encourage you to assess the operational core business values of Just Frames."

With that, Ed spoke up. He could see that Ben had captured Frank's attention. Ed shared about his experience with the dolphins, what they had learned from Trevor, and how Ben's input today was a direct benefit of his new Swim SidewayZ approach to leadership: of letting go so they all could grow.

He shared the values he had developed from his research, the dream about the dolphins, and how the values he had learned resonated with the spirit at Preston. He was committed to improving how leadership and management functioned within the company in order to be as innovative and adaptable as Frank was at Western.

Then Ed put a proposition to Frank: "I've always admired your business acumen, loyalty, and friendship, and I want you to know that I want your business, but I know more about my business than you do. I strongly encourage you to take a careful look at more than the bottom line of your deal with Just Frames; there is a double bottom line in this deal and the other one is about ethics and values. I'm no expert on the subject, but I know enough to say that I wouldn't hesitate to be in business with Western, and I think you feel the same about Preston."

Frank, without hesitation, confirmed that he shared Ed's perspective. Then Ed said, "Frank, please don't make a decision to merge with Just Frame's until you can be as sure about their character as you are about Preston's."

Frank sat speechless for what seemed like an eternity, then turned to Ben and said, "Young man, thank you for your question, and for challenging me to adopt a different decision approach. I will be giving a lot of thought to what was said here today. However, I do need to get to another appointment. Ed, let's get together at my house this weekend and talk about this more, and you too Ben, if you're free and if that's okay with Ed." Ben's eyes lit up. Ed said he thought that that was a swell idea.

On Saturday morning Ed drove over to Ben's house and picked him up for the drive to Frank's place. "Good morning, Ben," said Ed, as Ben fastened his seat belt.

"And good morning to you, too," said Ben.

"I certainly want to thank you for speaking up and sharing your ideas with Frank. You may have saved us from a fate that makes me shudder when I think of it."

"Well, it was nothing," said Ben earnestly. "A few weeks ago I probably wouldn't have said anything. I felt empowered to speak up thanks to you, or should I say thanks to you and the dolphins?" The men looked at each other, smiled, and nodded in unison.

The drive to Frank's house took about fifteen minutes. Along the way, Ed and Ben spoke about what Trevor had taught them and how their relationship had been changed since Ed's encounter with the dolphins. Subsequently, his willingness to share his story and incorporate what he had learned from them into his leadership approach had changed as well. They discussed that it was astonishing how people either discover or adopt a set of core values or beliefs as their own. They had believed all along that values were something people either chose or created, not that they had been available to them along.

Ed also mentioned to Ben how he now saw him in a new way and how grateful he felt to be benefiting from discovering and living out the value of inclusion. He mentioned that when Ben thanked him it resonated with him; that what he was actually being thanked for being an authentic leader. Additionally, he liked the effect he was experiencing, and the effect his leadership had had on his customers, both the outcome it produced at the meeting with Frank and, potentially, for the whole company. In that moment, he felt as if he had been rescued by his newly discovered values; no doubt Ben probably felt liberated.

Ed's tires rolling across the sparkling white aggregate covering Frank's expansive circular driveway announced his arrival. Soon the screen at the front door opened and down the steps Frank came to welcome them. "Mi casa es su casa," Frank said in perfect Spanish.

"Hey, I didn't know you spoke Spanish, Frank," said Ed.

"Yes, I studied it in high school and college, and with Spanish-speaking people fast becoming the majority population in California, I'm glad I did. Do you realize that more than half of my workforce speaks Spanish as their first language?"

Ed and Ben said nothing as they followed Frank into the house. Nevertheless, Ed filed that comment in his mind; it dawned on him that the demographics of his installation and fabrication crews were similar in comparison to what existed at Western.

"Marsha couldn't wait around to say hello, but she prepared this healthy breakfast for us before she left for her tennis lessons. That woman is always learning something new.

I got the inspiration to go after hotel and government business from watching the way she responded to her breast cancer diagnosis twenty years ago. I felt lost and terrified by the prospects of losing my wife; to be honest I wasn't much support to her. On that day she was holding me up! As I held my head down in sorrow, she put her arms around me and said, 'I'm going to beat this thing.' Then she shared an affirmation with me that her grandmother always repeated when she had to manage tough situations. She said, 'The key to having a happy life isn't trying to control what happens in your life, but how you respond when things happen.' Her response to having cancer was to learn as much as she could about the disease and in so doing she came across homeopathic books that encouraged patients to engage in learning new things that they are passionate about, and to develop healthy eating habits."

"Wow," said Ben, "I don't think I've ever eaten this healthy. I'm afraid to tell you what I usually have for breakfast."

"Ditto," said Ed, "but can you say more about how she influenced your strategy to go after a different market share, Frank?" Ed asked.

"Sure. I was stuck on the idea that you didn't fix something that wasn't broken. We were flush with cash and carried no debt; I wasn't thinking that the future would be anything different from the present. I felt the same way about our lives. In general, I never thought either one of us would get sick or that there was anything wrong with eating the food that we were eating; steak and burgers four to five times a week, pizza and fried chicken on the weekends. When she decided to change her diet, I thought I would do the same thing in order to support her. In the process, I lost thirty pounds and increased my energy.

When she began to embrace learning new things, I felt that we were drifting apart because she was devouring books. Sometimes she would read three or four a month; she was changing before my eyes. Researchers say that people who read ten books of 250 pages or more on the same subject become authorities on that topic. Suddenly, I found myself lying next to an expert. It made me feel lazy and inferior; I had always been the enterprising person in the family.

That's when I began to read some of the books she was reading so that we had something in common to talk about. One book in particular influenced my decision to pursue new markets. It was 'Leadership and the New Science,' by Margaret Wheaton. I learned that change was inevitable and something to embrace as a natural and necessary part of the regeneration of all living things, even the universe itself. The book helped me to think of Western and me as two inflexible elements amid an ever-changing environment. It became clear to me that I and the company were at risk of not being ready to respond to the changes that would take place in our industry."

Ed thanked Frank for sharing such a personal part of his life and then he said, "Happiness and success are truly tied to how we respond to events in our lives, including change. My dolphin experience drastically changed my approach to leadership, and hearing your and Marsha's stories, and seeing this healthy food, make me think that I also need to make some lifestyle changes," as he rubbed the part of his belly that lay over his waistband."

"Well guys, let's eat," said Frank.

"I like that idea!" said Ben.

As they sat down to eat, Frank talked about Ed's proposal. "I thought a lot about what you and Ben said and realized that I wasn't doing my due diligence in evaluating Just Frame's deal." Still harking back, Frank said, "and Ed, I had never heard the expression 'a double bottom line,' so when you mentioned it I needed some time to research the term. And I must say, I learned something very important."

"What was that?" asked Ed, as Frank paused.

"That I don't lead Western with an explicitly-stated set of core values and have never considered evaluating Just Frames against such a standard, or our own performance, for that matter."

Ben and Frank nodded supportively at Frank's admittance. "But when Ben made his point about the amount of business we do with Preston as opposed to the amount we have at Just Frames, I realized it was a fact I had never given any thought. So, over the last few days I sat down with my management team and asked them to list the reasons why we did business with Preston and Just Frames."

"What did you find out?" Ed inquired nervously, as he stopped eating to listen to Frank's reply.

Frank smiled and said, "The only reason Preston doesn't have all our business is because we have a policy that we don't give 100% of our business to any one vendor. However, after we looked closely at why we did the majority of our business with Preston, we learned you were always competitive on price, but more importantly, superior on quality, timeliness, and service.

What we concluded was that in doing this reflection, we saw a need to reconsider our vendor policy and that we had a need to be clear and explicit with our decision-making processes and, to your credit, and Ben's, we learned we had been violating my company values without even knowing it."

"What do you mean you were violating your company values without knowing it?" asked Ben quizzically.

"Everyone at Western knows that I try to operate by an unwritten principle that says all business decisions should be made based on what's in the best interest of the company. Clearly, not giving all my business to a vendor that so outperforms the competition reflects an antiquated policy, which doesn't align with our values.

Then Frank turned to Ben and said, "Would you think it impulsive of me if I said 'Ben, give me a call on Monday so that we can start on the paperwork for the government contract?'"

Ed smiled and looked at Ben, who gathered himself and answered through a mouth full of fruit salad, "No, I think it would be a good call, Frank." With that, all three of the men shook hands on the deal. They established a bond between them based on a common quest to live and work by ethical values.

As they concluded their meeting, Frank walked them to the car. While Ed and Ben fastened their seat belts, Frank walked back to the house, then suddenly pivoted and walked back to the car and motioned hurriedly for Ed to lower his window. Ed cautiously lowered the widow, somewhat concerned that maybe Frank had changed his mind about doing the deal, "Yeah, Frank?" he yelled back.

"Ed, I need a favor," Frank requested.

"Sure, anything Frank, whatcha need buddy?" replied Ed.

"Would you email me that consultant's name who is helping you with the values work?"

"Oh, you mean Trevor?"

"Yep. Send me his contact information, I would like to talk with him."

"Sure thing, buddy, I'll take care of it first thing Monday morning."

Chapter 6

Excited about winning the opportunity to fill Western's order for its government contract and moreover, the possibility of receiving 100% of their business in the future, Ed gleefully sent an email to team members asking them to convene for a meeting in the conference room on Monday morning. He mentioned in the message that he had spoken with Trevor Bradshaw, and notified him that the team was ready to move on to the next step in the process of learning to live by values. He felt as though he was walking on air for the whole weekend, and this feeling remained with him as he entered the conference room on Monday.

"Good to see you again, Ed," said Trevor, as he excused himself from talking with Brenda.

"You too, buddy," said Ed, enthusiastically. "I'm anxious to get started using the values."

"I'm glad to hear that, just let me know when you're ready for me to get started," said Trevor.

"Ok, will do. I just need to make a quick announcement to the team." With that, Ed called the meeting to order and with the biggest smile that could fit on his face, told the team what had happened at Frank's house over the weekend.

"So, does this mean no layoffs this year?" queried Brenda.

"Yes, it does," said Ed, as he gave a wink and the thumbs-up sign to the group. With that gesture, the team let out a huge cheer and an atta-boy to Ben for the comments he'd made to Frank. Ed made it clear to everyone that this deal wouldn't have happened without Ben's involvement and that we all owed him our thanks. With that, everyone, in the room walked up to Ben and gave him either a high five or a fist bump. Through customary shyness, Ben blushed bright red in the light of the accolades. Nonetheless, he was overjoyed with the recognition.

Ed thanked Ben but gave all the credit for his actions to his wife, Anne, and the dolphins. It was Anne who helped him to understand that his fear of vulnerability and need for control were keeping him from perceiving that his staff thought he didn't trust them. The truth was, he was ignorant of his behavior and fearful of the judgment of others. To the dolphins, he owed his greatest gratitude; it was from them that he learned that relying on others is a powerful and necessary element, and the strongest expression of teamwork.

As Ed finished his statement, Jim shouted through the applause, "You're a good man, thanks for being willing to embrace change."

"You're welcome, Jim," said Ed. Then Ed turned to the second item on the meeting agenda. "I'm sure you all remember the work we did with Trevor a couple of weeks ago. Well, I'm glad to announce that Trevor has accepted our request for him to help us implement our values. With that, Ed invited Trevor to the front of the room.

Trevor began the discussion by saying that he understood that their goal was to become a values-centric company, and that values centric companies use a set of core business values to govern the performance and behavior of all Stakeholders. In this way, values serve as a common language that coalesce and connect people for the benefit of all stakeholder groups. Using a model that he created to illustrate what a values-centric organization looks like, he explained that in a values-centric company, values can be thought of as a common set of beliefs that serve as a source of energy, illumination, and direction; similar to our sun.

He pointed to the word Values on his values centric model and said that his goal was to teach the group that every organization, like every person in the room, has a personality, which is a reflection of the organizational culture.

Trevor further explained that a company's personality consists of assumptions about things that happen on the inside, and the outside of it, that affect it in some way. Going further, he taught the group about the four functional areas of all organizations. Trevor mentioned that stakeholders are all of the people inside and outside the organization who depend on it for their economic viability, and in some cases a sense of belonging, identification, and life purpose. He explained that many people consider their workplace their home away from home, where

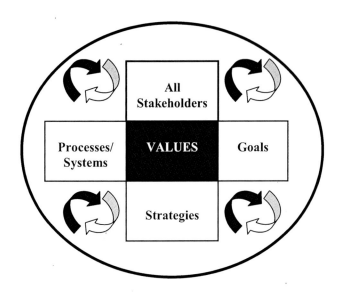

they have their closest friends, and where they feel valued. It is no wonder why mortality among early retirees is so disproportionately higher than those who work past retirement age.

He then turned to a discussion of Goals. He said that the most notable thing to remember about goals is that they are just dreams with a deadline. Trevor stressed the notion that organizations that function without clear and  measurable goals run the risk of becoming like the athlete who only talks about making the team rather than setting goals to measure whether any progress is being made for a spot on the roster. The wishful athlete will have no confident way of knowing whether he is making any progress towards preparing for the challenge that lies ahead. Like a dream, his efforts will be boundless and unstructured.

"That brings up a good question, Trevor," said Ed. "I thought you were talking about values. It sounds like you're saying that companies should be goal centric. I mean, what I think I hear you saying is that companies can't be successful unless they set goals." Trevor replied that what Ed said was partially true. He said that while goal setting is critical for success and effectiveness, they must be developed to align with the core values of the company.

"Any goal that doesn't align with the core values of a company should be reevaluated and reframed to meet this vital criterion, or you run the risk of being a company that is goal centric," Trevor said.

"And what is the problem with that?" asked Jim, quizzically.

Trevor responded anecdotally, "Imagine living as a family where values are ignored or subordinate to the family's goals, and that one of the goals is for the family to be the richest people in their county. By what principles would those parents raise their children? What might the relationship between the parents project? How would the children treat their friends and classmates? What would be their interest in spirituality?

"That doesn't make for a pretty picture," said Brenda. "That was a good example. I attended a private boarding school with girls who grew up in similar situations. They were some of the most impersonal and aggressive girls in school. They earned excellent grades and won most of the athletic and academic awards for performance, but none of the good citizenship awards. Overall, they didn't have any friends and were isolated by the other girls. I used to feel sorry for them; being labeled self-absorbed and snobbish seemed a terrible price to pay for success."

"I agree," said Trevor, "but companies unknowingly and some consciously make that decision all the time."

"Yep, they sure do," said Ed. "Like ours, I mean unknowingly that is … thank goodness for dolphins."

Trevor proceeded to discuss the third element in the model: Strategies. He explained that strategies were deliberate ideas about what direction a company believes it should be heading, and goal setting was a natural outpouring of good strategies. In other words, a goal would logically emerge from sound strategies as a way of measuring whether a particular strategy was working.

"Like the athlete, you spoke about," said Ben.

"Say more," said Trevor.

"Well, it didn't seem like the athlete had developed a prudent strategy for preparing to make the roster. I mean, the athlete had not set any goals; he just had a dream or wish, but not a clear way to assess progress."

"Bravo," said Trevor, "that's exactly what I mean!"

Putting one knee on the chair, Trevor taught the group that strategies are as much a product of the process as the results they achieve. "Every strategy asks key questions in order to come to a decision; what is our vision, what is our purpose, what is the challenge, and what is our capacity to meet or exceed the challenge."

There are many different strategic methods of achieving desired results, but they all share one common feature. They all encourage goal setting as a means of tracking performance."

"I understand where you're coming from with this Trevor," said Ed, "but what is the central reason from a business standpoint as to why goal setting is so important?"

"Simply put," Trevor replied, "goal setting enables you to know if you're nearing your desired result or falling short. This allows you to see if your strategy is working."

And with that knowledge you have the sense to change course, tweak your strategy, or jettison it all together in some cases."

"You mean like learning to Swim SidewayZ?" said Ed with a smile.

"You got it," said Trevor. "In the consulting world, we prefer to speak of companies that demonstrate that type of personality as 'change oriented.'"

Change oriented companies integrate change into their culture by making it a part of their value system at all levels. They learn that reacting to something that is inevitable creates unnecessary chaos, urgency, and anxiety; and that it's far better to embrace change as a natural and necessary force of life, which brings with it opportunities for new beginnings, renewal, and growth."

"But I always thought people hated change; that's what they taught us in graduate school," said Carl.

Trevor was expecting this since it was a customary response he heard from managers. He explained that, to the contrary, people value change more than anything else they experience. He went further to say that management's lack of transparency and inclusion causes the anxiety and resistance that people express.

"Ummm,"said Jim, "hold on there a minute. There's more to it than that. My people hate an idea that could mean they will have to give up something or do more work."

"Yes, that might be true," said Trevor. "Still, even people with that attitude are willing to accept those consequences when they get a chance to influence those outcomes from the outset. As if in consensus making, when their perspectives are respected, people are more willing to accept contrary decisions. In the big picture, there is more than mere pacification in true consensus making and inclusion. When the people involved are truly knowledgeable about the issues and facts of a situation, and the people responsible for making decisions are functioning according to core values that include participation, then what is shared will, to some meaningful degree, inform a decision. Especially, if it's clear how a decision will strengthen the processes and systems that people count on to get the work done," continued Trevor.

"Processes and Systems are probably one of the keys to the successful functionality of all companies," said Trevor. "At the end of the day, there are four things all successful companies must possess, talented, capable, and committed people; a strong culture; smart strategies; and efficient processes and systems. Processes and Systems are to the other three components what the human heart is to other parts of the body. The heart is a muscle that acts as a pump, delivering nutrients and oxygen-rich blood to all parts of the body, including the brain.

A company's processes and systems disseminate vital information that links and connects all stakeholders. They also play a critical role in providing companies with the order and discipline they need in order to repeat and study their performance. Poor Processes and Systems eventuate to weak results."

Trevor explained that being a value-centric company is about creating a way to stay aligned with your core values in order to build confidence into the stakeholders that the beliefs really do govern performance, behavior, and practices at all levels. He pointed to the small concentric arrows between each of the four elements in the model. They were indications of the role values have as a connective agent; that through the values stakeholders functioned with both self-governance and the confidence that there is a real sense of "connective consciousness" to all that goes on in the company.

Glancing at his watch, Trevor told the group, "My, we have been at this for three hours, how about a fifteen minute break."

"I thought you would never say it," said Ben.

As the group was preparing to leave the room, Ed asked Trevor a question. "Are we going to create some values in this session?"

"Well no, not exactly, Ed," said Trevor.

"Well, then what was the point of showing us the model," challenged Jim.

Smiling, Trevor said, "When you come back from your break I will teach you a very salient feature about values that will answer your questions and be a part of your consciousness all the days of your lives."

"Sounds as exciting as Ed's dolphin story," said Carl.

"Yeah, sure does," said Jim, jokingly.

"They are more similar than you could ever imagine," assured Trevor.

Chapter 7

"Welcome back folks, and thanks for returning on time," said Trevor, as the group settled in to their seats. He reconvened the meeting by answering Ed's question with a question. "Ed, what would you say was the most important thing you learned from the dolphins?"

Ed finished swallowing a sip of his coffee, reflected for a moment and said, "I would say it was their altruism."

Trevor smiled and turned to Jim and asked, "Jim, would you say that Ed created that value or discovered it?"

"I would say that it's obvious that he discovered it," answered Jim.

"Correct answer," said Trevor. Trevor proceeded to teach the group that values are not created but discovered, either through direct life experiences, or by others, or sometimes by dolphins.

"So, how can we discover our values at Preston?" said Brenda.

"That's a terrific question, but I'm not surprised you asked it, Brenda; it's what I expected from someone in HR," Trevor said through a smile.

Then he said that discovering their company values can begin with remembering that companies often function implicitly with their values. "Like all people, companies have values, some function with them explicitly and others implicitly. Those that function with them explicitly are conscious of them and integrate the values into their culture so that they have a purposeful effect on every level. In contrast, where values are not integrated in a conscious manner, they are there implicitly as the beliefs and principles of individuals or sometimes departments. Companies that function implicitly with their values are less productive, experiencing success serendipitously. In other words, for these companies, success occurs less consistently, or because of a strong market demand by just showing up."

My approach with assisting these companies at discovering their values involves asking them two questions: how did the company act during its most profitable years, and, if given a choice, what would people like to see change?" Trevor explained that the first question helped people to reflect on how they function and behave under ideal conditions. This approach was applied because it often uncovered values representative of how the company shared the fruits of its success with other stakeholder groups inside and outside of the company, and whether they valued the efficiency of their processes and systems. It also allowed for an assessment of how well they revisited their strategies and goals, in particular, whether their attitudes about spending and investing were different during times of abundance.

To lend some color to his discussion, Trevor told the group a story about a small financial firm that he had worked with. They had turned to a consultant to assist them with developing a set of core values as a transition strategy following the CEO's buyout of the three other company founders. The consultant smartly suggested this strategy because the company's culture was unhealthy; it was common for less productive people to be hazed or scrutinized about their religious beliefs and affiliations, or for women to be subjected to unfair treatment or sexual harassment.

In addition, the company was administratively immature. Nevertheless, they had prospered as a four-year-old start-up that grew into a company with earnings of $25 million and a profit of $12 million. They had accomplished this with the benefit of some very talented young people, visionary and courageous leadership, and phenomenal market demand.

Trevor said that by the time they retained him, they had been experiencing a downturn in the market and it was affecting their business. Lending to the CEO's concern were the new competitors whose youthful tenacity, intellectual capital, and entrepreneurial courage were matching their performance. These forces, compounded by the emergence of three disgruntled founders who maintained ties to key producers, which they used to deride the CEO, put a strain on the company culture and productivity.

The CEO had asked Trevor for advice in strengthening the company's climate. Turnover had been occurring in areas critical to the success of the company and he had been worrying that he could not survive if it continued. Exasperating the CEO's concerns was the fact that he had taken out a personal line of credit for $10 million dollars to buy out his partners. For the last two quarters the firm had suffered losses that were a bellwether of the worst year the firm would experience since its inception.

Trevor told the CEO that he wanted to interview members of the organization and ask them why they thought the firm was in its current state. The CEO gave him the green light. After four days, Trevor had completed the interviews and took the weekend to organize the data into a report he could review with the CEO. Three striking themes leaped out. First, people thought the CEO was not living by the values that he espoused. Second, non-revenue generating contributors felt management valued revenue producers more than it valued others. Thirdly, revenue producers no longer felt included in the decision-making process even though they were responsible for 60% of the firm's fiscal success.

Trevor told the CEO that it was his opinion that his firm was suffering from a classic case of leader "Assassination by Values." Trevor mentioned that the CEO looked at him with a puzzled expression and said, "What the heck does that mean," he said.

Trevor told the CEO that it appeared to him that as he goes, so goes his culture and the productivity of his company. He told him that people see him as a heroic leader and this is probably because he was willing to take personal risks at keeping the company whole while in a down market. In addition, while productivity had been down they viewed him as someone who turned things around with courage, vision, and innovation. Moreover, some were upset with him because he had chosen to function in a silo, and ironically, that he had given his attention only to high-revenue producers. In short, they were judging him with the exact values he had worked to discover. They were assassinating him with his company's core values.

Trevor told the group that the CEO felt challenged by that idea and told him that he felt like he was killing himself trying to keep his company afloat and his people were worried about him not including them and making them feel valued. He complained that they sounded like a bunch of spoiled children.

In that instance, Trevor told the team that he pointed to a poster on the CEO's office wall that listed the firm's core values, and asked him which of the values on the poster did he think were most pertinent to the firm, given what they were going through today. The CEO studied the list and told him financial stability, responsibility, and teamwork.

Trevor congratulated the CEO and told him that he had made good choices. Then Trevor explained to the CEO that if teamwork is crucial to the success of the firm, then why does he feel the need to exclude people from the decision-making process? The CEO explained that, upon reflection, he had not realized he was ignoring the importance of living out this value; he was shocked to learn this.

Sensing the CEO was distraught; Trevor told him that when the trajectory of a company's revenue generation needs correcting, it's common for a leader to be distracted by the churn created due to the urgency. He told him all understand the significance of revenue to the survival of a business. However, what most leaders must remember is that it is not what happens to you, but how you react to what happens that matters. Trevor smiled and told group that he was pleased when the CEO leaned forward and said to that what he had said made a lot sense and encouraged him to say more.

Trevor proceeded by explaining that, in the CEO's case, the thing to remember was that he was the standard-bearer and that all eyes were on him. The ship will sail in the direction he points as long as people believe that he is consistently using a protocol that they all agreed and understood.

The CEO confirmed to Trevor that he was buying into what he was trying to teach him when he commented that it was like functioning according to the values. Then the CEO threw his head back from the obvious implications of his statement.

To Trevor's delight, the CEO saw for himself that by living out the values, he could empower the team to solve their production problem. He stated to the CEO to just remember to teach the revenue producers to practice the same thing with the support staff that partners with them for the company's success. He said he called this The Chain of Influence. He told the CEO that he can influence revenue producers who in turn influence the support staff. By doing this, he could permeate the organization with diffused values. In this way, he would create a connective consciousness. As a result, people would govern themselves according to the same core values; in a sense, the firm would duplicate itself by its values. Then Trevor asked the CEO to consider Benoît Mandelbrot's fractal as a model of how this works.

Trevor powered up his laptop, opened a photo of Mandelbrot's fractal, and invited the group to gather around and observe. He explained that a fractal is a geometric shape that has the capacity to divide itself into additional smaller parts that resemble the whole. He explained that the firm was a representative whole of the experiences of all its stakeholders, which we understand as being its culture. The firm's culture is, for the most part, its values; the fractal model allows us a means of understanding when discovering our values and telling stories about them. We diffuse them in a constructive way and imbue the consciousness of others, who in turn adopt them, thereby replicating the values at every level of the firm.

The CEO told Trevor that the fractal metaphor made a lot of sense; and jokingly asked why he didn't know that.

Trevor assured him that he did know it, but that he had just stopped practicing it. He said that it was normal to retreat to one's comfort zone under

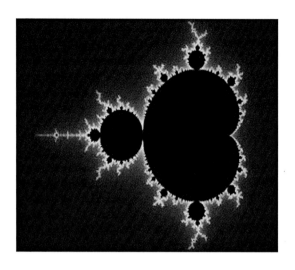

stress. He told the CEO that he was an entrepreneur. Working in a silo was something he knew; he just had to remember to share this task with other stakeholders. After all, their talents, skills, and commitment to assist him with achieving the mission and goals of the company were the reasons why he hired them. Since he was facing hard times, he had to remember this truth and discipline himself to live by the company's values in both the good and tough times. It is not easy to do, but the CEO discovered his values and Trevor hoped that they were the essence of what his firm believed about itself, Trevor said rhetorically and then paused.

The CEO, compelled by the significance of the statement, interjected that they were what his company believed and that they were truly representative of what he and his people stood for. He emphasized that the onus was on him and reaffirmed Trevor's belief that being a standard-bearer was what it meant to live by their core values.

Trevor told the CEO that he was unequivocally correct. At that, the CEO asked for Trevor's help and Trevor told him that he would be glad to be his coach.

Trevor told the group that he worked with the CEO for four years, and in spite of some tough markets, they regained their position as a leader in their industry. The CEO became a model of what it meant to be a values standard-bearer. He planned weekly huddles with the entire company at breakfast meetings with his top producers, at which time he used one of the core values as a strategy to guide discussion, further establish a common language, and integrate the values with the company's practices.

This approach encouraged staff participation and provided a common means to govern behavior in meetings and daily practices. The approach also encouraged others to engage in discussions, which leveraged the diversity of ideas, and more powerfully, they influenced the CEO to use many of the suggestions to improve sales and marketing strategies. Consultants conducted sexual harassment training, cultural sensitivity training, and communication competency skills training and coaching.

"Sounds as if they were doing a little bit of 'Swimming SidewayZ' to me, Ed," chimed Carl.

Ed smiled and said, "You think?"

"You betcha they were. They swam themselves into becoming a better-managed company because the CEO let the values govern every stroke he took for the rest of his career," said Trevor.

"Hey, I like that metaphor," realizing that it was appropriate for describing the behavior of his client. "Thanks for sharing that story, Trevor," said Ed. "I know the point of the story was to address me and Jim's question about where values come from, but I gleaned a bit more from it."

"Please say more," said Trevor.

"Alright," said, Ed. "It made me think that I've been functioning in a silo my entire career."

"Well, do you know why you chose that style of leadership?" said Brenda.

"Yeah, I do. My dad and my surrogate uncle were my mentors and role models growing up, and they both had truly independent and introverted personalities and functioned as such in their businesses. They would do anything in the world to help someone, but they wanted to do everything themselves. In fact, my uncle agonized over whether to use my strategy that was responsible for the growth of the company."

"It's not easy to think outside of a mental frame," said Trevor. "Mental frames are mental constructs that cognitive psychologists believe are at the core of a person's perception of the world; it can take a long time before someone is able to change how he thinks about a thing, person, or his own behavior for that matter."

"Well, then how do you explain Ed's sudden shift in behavior to include us in helping him to lead Preston?" asked Ben, respectfully.

"Well, Ed may be the best person to answer that question, but if I had to guess, I would say that the experience he had with the dolphins probably was what psychotherapists call an event jolt; a life-changing experience that broke through the do-it-yourself values frame he adopted from his dad and uncle." Ed said that that was a very insightful explanation. While he didn't have a rationalization for why the shift occurred, he simply knew that he felt compelled to lead differently than he had in the past and that working in isolation was suddenly no longer an option.

"Thanks for that honest answer, Ed," said Trevor. "Now I know why Jim said '… if you know Ed, you know he isn't the type to make up stories. If he tells you something you can bet it's the truth, and he has given a lot of thought to it.' I think this is an excellent time for us to begin discovering the core values at Preston." With that, Trevor went to the flip chart and wrote the first question in large, bold letters:

How did the company act during its
most profitable years?

The group reflected on the question for a few minutes, and then someone spoke up. "Honestly," said Jim, "we spent a lot of money on things without giving much thought to how it was going to benefit us or what need it was going to fulfill. No offense Ed, but the books reflect many expenses you requisitioned without any of us every talking about them in management meetings."

The corners of Ed's mouth drooped as he said, "I'm sure I've done a lot of that Jim. Thinking of ways to improve the company occupied me whenever things were going well. Nevertheless, as I sit here I realize that many of those ideas have never been fully thought out. Not that I didn't give thought to them, but I obviously didn't test my ideas in the minds of my team."

Jim proceeded to tell Ed how much he appreciated what he had to say, because he hoped it meant he had the right to challenge him about requisitions in the future.

Ed assured him that was the case, and better, that maybe Trevor could show them some decision making methods that could assist them in achieving that result.

"That won't be a problem," said Trevor. "It sounds to me like you may have uncovered a potential core value," he said as he went to the flip chart and wrote:

Teaming Together to Make Strategic Decisions!

"Ha, I remember this exercise now," said Brenda, recalling what Trevor did at her previous job.

"Ok, Brenda let's have it," said Trevor, gripping the marker between his fingers.

Brenda talked with the group about the charitable work the company does when it reaches its revenue goals. She told stories about the money and gifts Preston gives to the ministries to support homeless programs, fundraisers to find a cure for AIDS,  habitat development projects in Mexico, and other social programs to benefit people less fortunate. "Ed is always on us to do something to help youth in the surrounding community who are living impoverished lives," said Carl.

"Yeah, one Christmas Eve, he even called me, demanding that I meet him in the parking lot, in a real rough community, so that I could help him pass out toys and food to youth and their families. I never forgot that. I was upset that I was leaving my family to go out and help strangers, but I must admit, it taught me a lot about what is authentic about Christmas."

"And what is that," said Trevor, as he rested the marker on his chin.

"That it's not what you have or receive, but what you're prepared to give away to others," said Jim reflectively.

Reflecting on what Brenda and Jim had said, Trevor asked the group to identify the values espoused. Then he waited at the flip chart for one of them to respond. Within a few minutes, Jim said, "An unselfish concern for others."

"Thanks, Jim, that was very insightful," said Trevor.

Placing the cap back on the head of the marker Trevor stood quietly as he waited for someone else to offer up another story. After a few seconds, Ed spoke up.

"I agree that I've always made key decisions for the company without seeking the input of others, and for that, I apologize; it was a poor leadership practice, and inconsiderate of me given the talent available in this room, and within the company. Nevertheless, I believe I've done an admirable job over the years of being smart in the strategies I used to develop value for the company in many different markets. Though I didn't do a very good job of responding to this one," Ed said a bit contritely.

"We all make mistakes, Ed," said Ben. Smiling, he continued, "Someone once said it's not what happens to you that counts but how you respond to what happens. I'm proud to have had you as my boss over the years, Ed, and even more so in the last couple of weeks.

"It sounds as if we may have discovered two values this time," said Jim and Carl simultaneously, as the group broke out into a light chuckle.

"Who wants to go first?" asked Trevor through a smile.

"I'll give it a shot," said Jim, as Trevor flipped the marker into the air like a baton, caught it in his hand, removed the cap, and readied himself at the flip chart.

Responding accordingly is what matters.

"Hey, that is what I was going to say. Oh well, here is my second interpretation," sighed Carl, comically.

Trust starts with allowing for mistakes.

The first question Trevor asked was serving its purpose; the group was discovering its values and, in addition, sharing stories that illuminated the rich relationships they had created between themselves. Trevor taught the group that the power of storytelling helps people get in touch with what is noteworthy in their lives. Often, what they discover is that relationships are the most powerful constant in their experiences at work and life; values are the central element connecting them to others. Then he wrote the second facilitative question on the flip chart.

If given a choice, what would people
like to see the company
change about itself?

"Well, I don't want to overcook the chicken, but I think the thing that needed to change the most was Ed's leadership style, and that train has already left the station," said Jim emphatically. Many heads in that room nodded affirmatively.

Trevor said, "Ok, well said. You have just uncovered another value." Jim's comment surprised the group; they had not said much, but as they reflected, Trevor went to the flip chart and wrote:

Leaders are responsible for setting direction
and being the standard-bearers of
the strategic plan.

"That was pretty astute of you, Trevor. I can see why you would say that. As you said before, leaders are the standard-bearers of the values; if we're going to be a values centric company then Ed has to live by the values," said Carl.

"Well, I think Trevor is saying more than that. I think there's a deeper message. I believe the message is that everyone in this room is a standard-bearer of the values," said Ed.

Trevor nodded his head confidently and, smiling to reinforce the point, said, "You're all in this together. Ed took the most important step when he began to swim SidewayZ in participating with you in this process and he has to continue in that posture. However, where the staff is concerned, you're all in this together unless you can demonstrate that you won't be able to change from a goal-centric to a values-centric company. Remember, like the fractal model, you're all now a reflection of Ed's decision to lead differently and all your direct reports will be reflections of your decision to be followers."

"That makes a lot of sense," said Ben.

"But is it that simple?" said Jim.

Trevor told the group there would be nothing simple about their journey. He reminded them they were in the first phase of a four-step process to achieve their objective. With that, he wrote the four steps on the flip chart:

1. Accept the idea that change is required and take appropriate and responsible action to do it.
2. Discover core values that are reflective of your experiences or that represent your desired state.
3. Develop a method of disseminating and embedding the values into the culture and among all stakeholders through an approach that is disciplined, transparent, organized, and consistent.
4. Build accountability at every level for standard-bearers and others.

Trevor explained to the group that because of Ed's courage to shift his leadership style and their willingness to forgive him and follow in the new direction, they had successfully launched their journey. They were now engrossed in the second step of the process of discovering their values. When Trevor finished his sentence, it dawned on him that the group had not answered the second facilitative question, so he revisited it by saying, "My experience tells me that it's often difficult for people to discuss the negative aspects about their own performance." Trevor took the cap off the marker, underlined the word people, asked the group to look more closely at the question, and waited for the group to respond. When no one spoke up, he prompted the group by asking. "Do you think your reticence is because you don't know what people are thinking?"

The group fell into a revealing silence. No one in the room moved as much as a muscle and Trevor realized he had hit a nerve. He had seen this before and it made a lot of sense. The group was suffering from a lack of leadership/management development and it was the consequence of Ed not seeking out their opinions and ideas. Consequently, it wasn't their practice to do it with others.

Action Steps

1. Survey other stakeholders to assess their opinions, comments, and suggestions about the core values.

2. Develop an ombudsperson to coach and mediate on values conflicts.

3. Develop a committee to recognize and reward people who live by the core values.

It was a negative fractal; they were reflecting Ed's leadership deficiencies. Trevor told them this and suggested they tackle this problem by asking people what they thought. He explained that they would simply include this question in the next phase of his plan in helping them to discover the core values. Trevor went to the flip chart and wrote the three action steps required for confirming the authenticity of the group's values and for uncovering what staff thought needed to change.

This thought was in his consciousness when Trevor said, "It will be interesting to learn what staff will contribute and if theirs match yours. Ed may be onto something. It would be the first time I facilitated the discovery of values that were in some way influenced by magical dolphins.

Possible learning points to build on

How would your organization answer these questions?

How do we behave when we are doing well as a business?

In what way would people in our organization say we should change?

Is management willing to be standard-bearers of the core values?

Chapter 8

Two days had passed since Ed and the group met with Trevor to discover Preston's core values. Now Trevor was back to assist them in further defining the values so they could be used in a survey to assess staff attitudes.

Trevor greeted the group as they streamed into the room, "Good to see you folks again, I've missed you," he said, spreading his arms wide.

"Good to see you, too," said Jim.

"Ditto," said Carl.

Trevor began the session by asking the group if anyone had any values updates they wanted to share.

Brenda asked, "What do you mean by that?"

Trevor clarified his question, "What I mean is, did you have any experiences or observe any events where the values were being practiced?"

"Funny you should ask," said Carl. "I did notice that I was more conscious of the values and, as a result, I did observe my staff **Teaming Together to Make Strategic Decisions**. We couldn't figure out why the gas injection applicator that we use to insert gas between windowpanes wasn't functioning properly. We were a bit stressed because the windows were Western's first order for their new government contract." Ed's eyebrows rose a bit when he heard those words.

Carl proceeded with telling his story by telling the group that after an hour or so a maintenance crewmember, who has been employed with Preston for 15 years, asked if he could offer the crew a suggestion. I eaves dropped on their conversation from my office on the production floor. The maintenance worker explained to the crew that he thought the injector head probably needed cleaning. When they asked him why he thought so, he said he had worked overtime during the weekend and thought the new vendor hired to clean the heads had done a poor job. When the crew inspected the heads they discovered the maintenance worker was correct in his assessment. They asked him why he hadn't mentioned anything. He stated that no one had ever asked his opinion before, so he didn't think anyone would be interested.

I immediately went on the floor to speak to my manager and have him arrange a meeting with the repairperson's supervisor to let him know of the poor service we received. I also told him that we would be doing a better job of including people at all levels in our department meetings and empowering them to report things that are inconsistent with our goals and values.

He then replied, "What values are you talking about, Carl?"

"I understood in that moment just how valuable discovering and living by values were to the effectiveness and strength of our company."

"That was very insightful, Carl" said Trevor.

"So what is the status of the order now?" Ed inquired.

"Don't fret Ed. We're going to be right on time!" said Carl.

"Thanks," said Ed. Trevor proceeded by commending Carl for the way he handled the situation, especially his involvement of the supervisor and acknowledgement of the maintenance worker's contribution.

Trevor said to the group, "As you can see, we can gain much from being conscious of values functioning under the surface." He went on to say that it was marvelous that the maintenance worker had decided to act on his own values and that his values had aligned with the required action. However, this was succeeding by accident, which wasn't a reliable way of achieving long-term success.

The next step in the process of living by values would be to normalize and embed the values in Preston's culture, which would provide a more reliable means of producing desired results.

Trevor spun around on the balls of his feet, displaying some of the athleticism that made him an All-Ivy league tennis player. He went to the flip chat and wrote, "**Operationalizing the Core Values**." He explained that this was the next step in embedding the values in Preston's culture. The first task in accomplishing this was to identify goals for each of the core values; he called these goals **Intended Results**. As he wrote this on the flip chart, Trevor explained that these were criteria for developing a common language for living by their core values; **Succinct, Clear, Practical, and Measurable Sentences and Phrases**. The benefit of this was that people would know what the overarching goals were for achieving the values. He went on using the same criteria but with one exception, the addition of **Action**; the group would need to develop what he  coined "**The Behavioral Compasses.**"

"What are you going to do, take us on a hike?" said Jim, jokingly.

"Well, that's not a bad idea; wilderness survival activities are great for team building!" Trevor explained to the group that he was only kidding, but told them that the compasses were to serve much the same purpose as actual compasses do. While an actual compass can point us in the right direction when we begin a hike, it can also assist us in locating the right direction after unseen events force us off our path.

Over the next two weeks, Trevor worked with the group to develop one intended result and four behavioral compasses to support each of the five core values. When they had completed developing the values, Trevor listed them on clean flip charts.

Core Value:

Teaming together to make strategic decisions.

Intended Result:

To develop effective strategies through collaborating and respecting the input of others when making decisions that will affect all stakeholders.

Behavioral Compass:

- We solicit the input of others we work with to achieve best results.
- We strive to achieve healthy consensus in all our collective decisions.
- We make a conscious effort to gain input from a representative sample of all areas of the company for decisions that will affect all stakeholders.
- We employ transparency in reporting back team members about the process and rationale for all collaborative decisions.

Core Value:

Unselfish concern for others.

Intended Result:

To demonstrate a genuine consideration for the success and happiness of other stakeholders without being motivated by the pursuit of personal gain or recognition.

The Behavioral Compass:

- We proactively seek opportunities to support the success of others.
- We promote and celebrate the achievements and best efforts of other.
- We are honest and courteous about our observations and interpretations regarding the efforts of others.
- We offer others an opportunity to fulfill their need for reciprocity by being open to their assistance when their support is warranted.

Core Value:

Responding accordingly is what matters most.

Intended Result:

To demonstrate consistent, disciplined, and prudent thinking and controlled actions in the face of tough situations when experiencing stellar results.

The Behavioral Compass:

- We practice sound discipline during successful and challenging times in order to develop our best practices. We refer to our core values in an orderly and timely manner in order to strengthen alignment with our principles and ethics.
- We are mindful of and accountable to the goals and objectives we use to measure our financial performance and make efforts to adjust our actions when necessary in order to achieve them.
- We solicit, then listen to the opinions and concerns of all our stakeholders and respond appropriately and in a concerted way as individuals.

Core Value:

Trust starts with allowing for mistakes.

Intended Result:

To be smart in managing mistakes as learning opportunities for employee development, strengthening self and team trust, and confidence.

The Behavioral Compass:

- We promote an environment of career-long learning by supporting the right to learn from our mistakes that result from earnest efforts.
- We acknowledge and reward efforts that generate productive results from mistakes.
- We promote open and direct dialogue about team performance challenges within our groups, teams, and individual partnerships.
- We foster a climate of trust by offering forgiveness for earnest apologizes for behavior inconsistent with our values and principles.

Core Value:

Leaders are responsible for setting direction and being the standard-bearers of Preston's strategic plan.

Intended Result:

To develop leadership at every level that models Preston's core values in fulfilling its vision, mission, and goals.

The Behavioral Compass:

- We all accept the charge to self-govern according to the company's core values by referring to them to assess all of our practices and actions.
- We all recognize and accept that we are accountable to one another for living out our core values in an attempt to fulfill our vision, mission, and goals.
- We all reflect through our actions, the core values of our company to our external stakeholders in ways that esteem our mission and vision.
- We all embrace change as a necessary ingredient of self and organizational improvement and are ever observant of forces that teach us how to ready ourselves for living in the future.

While the group was reviewing the sum of their work, Trevor spoke with them about the survey he developed to gather input from staff about any suggestions or comments they had about the values. He distributed a copy of the survey to the members of the management team for their review.

"Ok, I really like this approach, Trevor," said Ed, with a sense of revelation. "In fact, it's our first step toward operationalizing our core values:

We make a conscious effort to gain input from a representative sample of all areas of the company for decisions that will affect all stakeholders.

"You got it, Ed! Boy, you're a fast learner," said Trevor.

"I can't say I was doing that consciously, so thanks for pointing that out to us," said Ed.

"That was very astute of you," Trevor said.

"The way you have shifted your leadership style in the short time since you had the experience with the dolphins confirms a belief I've always had about you, that you always had a heart for leading by values but lacked the knowhow," encouraged Bennington.

"Why, I appreciate that Ben, but it's a bit late in coming don't you think? I mean, I have a lot of catching up to do to make up for keeping you folks out of my decision making process."

"To the contrary, Ed. Remember we're all in this together. One of our values states, '**Trust starts with allowing for mistakes.**' Besides, one of the compasses supporting this value proclaims, '**We foster a climate of trust by offering forgiveness for earnest apologies for behavior inconsistent with our values and principles**.' I think that from the day you spoke of your dolphin adventure you were making an earnest apology for your behavior. Now you just have to Swim SidewayZ by learning to accept compliments," said Ben, with a smile.

"Well, of course you're right Ben, and I appreciate and acknowledge what you said. I've always thought my heart was in the right place, I just didn't always know how to connect it to my actions."

"That's a key discovery," said Trevor, "because living by values is all about having a way to be accountable to yourself and others who share the same principles and beliefs. It's about aligning the informed conscience with the appropriate actions. When you're all conscious of the values and have the trust that they all are accountable to them, the company will be transformed and empowered to achieve its mission. This is possible only when we possess the power to live out the values in a collective way."

The group was well on its way to introducing the values to the other internal stakeholders now that they had approved the structure of the values. Trevor explained that the next step was for him to email the survey to Brenda so that she and her staff could make some minor adjustments and circulate them to everyone, along with a cover letter explaining the purpose of the survey.

Trevor explained to Brenda that she should stress in the letter that it was management's intention to transform Preston into a company that valued inclusion and that seeking their input about the values was the first step toward fulfilling that objective. He also said it should inform the staff that management would be organizing a series of staff focus groups to report the results of the survey back to management and to discuss the findings in more detail. This would help to identify some gaps and eventually create action plans to reduce them.

With the values and survey ready for distribution, Trevor asked whether there were any questions or takeaways from the work they had accomplished over the week. The group reflected for a while and then Jim spoke up.

"This was a great activity, Trevor. If you were as good at tennis as you are at helping people discover their values, then you must have been one heck of a player."

"Thanks, Jim," said Trevor, blushing.

"I have a takeaway," said Ed. "The story Carl told about the involvement of the maintenance crew member spoke volumes about how important it is to create a culture of inclusion and empowerment. It makes me sad that I haven't developed a culture where people feel like their opinions are valued. If you want people to be a part of what you do, you have to invite their input and then recognize and reward it. I must learn to Swim SidewayZ in achieving this for Preston."

"Wrong," said Brenda, "we must Swim SidewayZ."

"Correct you are, Brenda, correct you are," said Ed joyfully.

Chapter 9

Working in tandem, Trevor and Brenda administered the survey company wide. The organization was abuzz with excitement and some caution as they came together in groups to complete the survey. People commented to Brenda and their managers that they appreciated the opportunity to participate in this groundbreaking event. In the cover letter introducing the survey, they mentioned that the survey was for improving the management of the company, and that the results of the survey would be reported to staff. This was something they found encouraging; it was the type of transparency needed to feel included.

When Brenda mentioned this to Ed, he shouted, "Now that is what Swimming SidewayZ will do for you," while letting out a loud chuckle. "Well, ok, what's next?" asked Ed, enthusiastically.

"Trevor will need to organize the data and reconvene the management team to review it and then roll it out to the rest of the company in focus groups. Comments should be collected and reported back to management and staff in a written report; I'm thinking it will take about two weeks to complete the process. Afterwards, Trevor will facilitate a strategy session with the management and a selected member from each of the focus groups," said Brenda.

"Wow, he is actually taking this inclusion process to another level," said Ed.

"Yep." said Brenda confidently, "If we're going to live by our values we will need change agents at every level."

"I guess I still have a long way to go with accepting inclusion at all levels to the degree Trevor is suggesting," muddled Ed.

"If you have any reservations with including people at every level, just remember how much we benefited from Ben's participation with bringing in the Western deal," said Brenda.

Frustrated with his inability to absorb the big picture, Ed grabbed the back of his neck, leaned back in his chair, and sighed in frustration with himself.

Noticing his frustration, Brenda tried to help. "Don't go beating yourself up over this Ed, you're doing a terrific job. After all, we wouldn't be this far down the path to changing our culture without your courage to change your leadership style. You're doing a fantastic job Swimming SidewayZ. Just remember, letting people participate in your processes is new to you. There will be more times when you will doubt this is the right thing to do; not everything will be as euphoric as the Ben situation or the bonds we created as a management team in these few weeks we have worked with Trevor. There will be challenges and struggles as we work to live out these values."

When you get stressed by the process and think of reverting back to a less transparent and more insulated approach, remember the event that led you to reconsider changing your leadership style."

"You mean the fact that I was saved by dolphins?" Ed asked, bringing his eyes down from the ceiling to meet Brenda's.

"No, not exactly," said Brenda, as she grabbed a pen and wrote her thoughts on a note pad and showed them to Ed.

In one way or another everything in the world is connected, there is no internal or external environment. Everything and everyone is dependent on something for his existence, survival, and success.

Everyone deserves a second chance to get things right!

Ed smiled and, glancing at the floor, said; "Now, that's very profound. I've heard that statement before; is it something Trevor taught us?"

"No, a very wise and courageous leader taught me the meaning of those words with his actions to transform his company by sharing a story about magical dolphins," said Brenda. Ed closed his eyes and nodded his head forward acknowledging the recognition of himself as the author of the statement.

"Thanks, Brenda. I needed to be reminded of that. We are all in this together and we all should have some say in what we need to do and how we get it done," said Ed, committing himself to Trevor's strategy.

"Okay, let's push forward and get it done. I'm going to learn to be more inclusive and transparent with how I lead this company, even if I have to die trying!"

"I'm on it, Ed," said Brenda smiling. "Now, don't go kicking the bucket after those dolphins went out of their way to drag you to shore. I will contact Trevor tomorrow to let him know we're all set," said Brenda.

"Ok, you're on a roll," said Ed. "I'll make it my business not to let that happen. Besides, I'm curious to see how effective we'll be at rolling this out company wide," said Ed.

"Good enough, boss. I will keep you in the loop as things unfold," said Brenda.

Brenda was just a day off with her prediction about when she and Trevor would have the survey data organized and prepared for review by the management team. The group came together for three hours to discuss the results and to learn how Trevor and Brenda planned to facilitate the focus groups. It was the staff's opinion that the management team had done an excellent job of identifying values, intended outcomes, and compasses that reflected their beliefs about what the culture should be at Preston. On the other hand, they didn't agree that management, or in some cases, their peers had done a very good job of living by the values.

This wasn't surprising to anyone, especially Trevor, who had cautioned the group not to expect the staff's agreement on many of these. Still, it was a valid exercise to see what people thought in order to establish a benchmark for the future. Everyone agreed with Trevor, while holding onto a general feeling of regret about the results.

Trevor set up PowerPoint slides with the results and turned the group's attention to the projection screen to discuss the results of the survey. Trevor directed the laser pointer to the column heading, **Keep**, and said, "It appears that staff is for keeping all the suggestions that the management team has made."

"Is that a good thing?" said Carl.

"I think so, but we'll have to understand why they came to these conclusions after we meet with the focus groups. For now it's suggested that staff believe you're representing what is indicative of their beliefs about what is and should be the culture at Preston."

"I think it says something more than that," said Brenda.

"Go on, Brenda," said Trevor.

"I think because these results are the average responses of staff, they are sending us a message that we're very much in tune with what they feel and need from us as leaders. I have a better understanding of what you meant when you said that we'd better be sure we're prepared to be standard bearers of the values. Now that we have done a good job of reflecting the values of the staff, they surely will be expecting us to live by them."

"I got that message as well. This result is extraordinarily revealing," said Jim, as he took notes.

Trevor agreed with the group and added that it was not unusual for the employees of a company this size to respond to a question with such consistency. He was eager to meet with the focus groups to see if there was anything more revealing behind the results.

Next, Trevor placed the laser on the column, **Needs to improve.** In all, there were 12 compasses that staff thought required improvement. In other words, it was the staff's perception that, as an organization, their performance and actions didn't align with these beliefs.

Ed was a bit troubled by these results and asked Trevor, "so, how do we begin to fix this?"

"Well, one of the strategies will be to get some clarity about the nature of the gaps," said Trevor. "I'm interested in knowing the Whys and Hows around these results. In other words, why have they come to these conclusions and how are they affecting them and their performance? I think once we know the answers to these questions we can have an intelligent discussion about what actions to take to achieve values alignment."

"Well, how long will it take?" asked Ed, anxiously.

"Well, to get clarity shouldn't take too long since I believe the results and the strong participation in the survey indicate people trust the process. Therefore, I think their responses are honest and accurate. Reducing the gaps is a different matter all together. Regardless of the type of gap, all the following elements will be required," said Trevor, as he grabbed a dry marker and wrote on the board.

Six Elements of Gap Reduction

1. Use accurate diagnosis to identify the gaps.

2. Use smart planning to set clear direction.

3. Ensure high morale for the required amount of human energy.

4. Provide strong capacity (human talent, infrastructure, and financial viability) and resources to support the process.

5. Develop smart strategies for responding to uncertainty and change.

6. Deliver strong operational performance to ensure thorough and reliable implementation and sustainability.

"Wow, I like the structure of this process. Is it to be used in the order you've presented them in, and should it be employed as steps?" queried Ed.

"For the most part, I would say yes," said Trevor, "but not necessarily as steps in the classic sense. Some items are actions with processes that need to be performed in order, like in the case of items 1, 2, 5, and 6. For the other items, if management can say with a high-level of confidence, backed by evidence, that the items are at the optimum level, then the item doesn't have to be included sequentially, as a process."

"Hey, that makes a lot of sense to me," said Brenda.

"I like how that works," said Ben. "I mean, on the one hand it's a sequential process that you can rely on for structure, but, on the other hand, it allows for flexibility by leaving it up to management to assess the readiness of certain items."

"And why is that a benefit?" asked Jim.

"Well, because it incorporates a human element that is reflective of experience we as leaders should be accountable to. I mean, I should be aware of my staff's morale, and likewise, I darn well should know if we have the capacity to get the job done." Ed raised his eyebrows and shook his head in the affirmative at Ben's comments.

Trevor smiled and said, "Ok, now, folks, I think you're on top of your game! I like what I'm hearing. How would you describe your growth in awareness since you began the process of becoming values centric?"

In unison, they shouted, "We are Swimming SidewayZ!" With that, they all let out a laugh!

"Ok, we have about an hour left, so let's use the time to review the last columns with responses." Trevor placed the laser on the column, **Strengths**.

"Ok, seems like we're doing some things right," said Jim.

"Well, yes, it seems that way. In fact you're probably doing more things right than you realize, and the same can be said for areas requiring improvement. The objective here isn't only to know but to know why!" said Trevor instructively.

CORE VALUE Teaming together to make strategic decisions					
	Strengths	Needs to improve	Keep	Change	Can't say
Current status:		X			
Intended Result: To develop effective strategies through collaborating and respecting the input of others when making decisions that will affect all stakeholders.		X			
Behavioral Compass: • We solicit the input of others.		X	X		
• We work with others to achieve the best results.		X	X		
• We strive to achieve healthy consensus in all our collective decisions.		X	X		
• We make a conscious effort to gain input from a representative sample of all areas of the company for decisions that will affect all stakeholders.		X	X		
• We employ transparency in reporting back to team members the process and rationale for all collaborative decisions		X	X		

CORE VALUE Unselfish concern for others					
	Strengths	Needs to improve	Keep	Change	Can't say
Current status:	X		X		
Intended result: To demonstrate a genuine consideration for the success and happiness of other stakeholders without being motivated by the pursuit for personal gain or recognition.	X		X		
Behavioral Compass: • We proactively seek opportunities to support the success of others.		X	X		
• We promote and celebrate the achievements and best efforts of others.	X	X	X		
• We are honest and courteous about our observations and interpretations regarding the efforts of others.	X		X		
• We offer others an opportunity to fulfill their need for reciprocity by being open to their assistance when their support is warranted.		X	X		

	Strengths	Needs to improve	Keep	Change	Can't say
CORE VALUE **Responding accordingly is what matters most**					
Current status:			X		
Intended Result: To demonstrate consistent, disciplined, and prudent thinking and actions in the face of tough situations and when experiencing stellar results			X		
Behavioral Compass: • We practice sound discipline during successful and challenging times in order to develop our best practices.	X		X		X
• We refer to our core values in an orderly and timely manner in order to strengthen alignment with our principles and ethics.		X	X		
• We are mindful of, and accountable, to the goals and objectives we use to measure our financial performance and make efforts to adjust our actions when necessary in order to achieve them	X		X		
• We solicit, then listen to the opinions and concerns of all our stakeholders and respond appropriately as individuals and in a concerted way		X	X		X

CORE VALUE Trust starts with allowing for mistakes					
	Strengths	Needs to improve	Keep	Change	Can't say
Current status:			X		
Intended Result: To be smart in managing mistakes as learning opportunities for personnel development, and strengthening self and team trust and confidence.			X		
Behavioral Compass: • We promote an environment of career long learning by supporting the right to learn from our mistakes that are the results of earnest efforts.		X	X		
• We acknowledge and reward efforts that transform mistakes into positive and productive results					X
• We promote open and direct dialogue about team performance challenges within our groups, teams, and individual partnerships		X	X		X
• We foster a climate of trust by offering forgiveness for earnest apologizes for behavior inconsistent with our values and principles			X		

	Strengths	Needs to improve	Keep	Change	Can't say
CORE VALUE **Leaders are responsible for setting direction and being the standard bearers of Preston's strategic plan**					
Current status:			X		
Intended Result: To develop leadership at every level that models Preston's core values in fulfilling its vision, mission, and goals.			X		
Behavioral Compass: • We govern ourselves according to our core values by referring to them to assess all of our practices and actions.			X		X
• We recognize and accept that we are accountable to one another for living our core values in an attempt to fulfill our vision, mission, and goals.			X		X
• We reflect through our actions the core values of our company to our external stakeholders in ways that esteem our mission and vision.			X		X
• We all embrace change as a necessary ingredient of self and organizational improvement and are ever observant of forces that teach us how to ready ourselves for living in the future.			X		X

"So what will be your objective in the focus group for these responses?" asked Ben.

"Good question," said Trevor.

"Brenda and I will use the same strategic approach as with the improvement results. We want to uncover the Whys and the Hows. Regarding the latter, we will aim to discover how staff believes these strengths can be used to improve performance and culture for themselves and the company."

"You seem to put a lot of emphasis on recognizing and taking advantage of strengths," said Ed. "Could you tell us why? I was raised to focus on improving weaknesses and not to waste too much time on what you already know how to do."

"I would be happy to do that. There are three important reasons why I believe knowing and building on your strengths are fundamental to the success of an organization," said Trevor, as he grabbed the dry eraser and began to write his thoughts on the board.

"Hey, you're pretty smart for a former jock," said Jim, jokingly, evoking a laugh from the group.

"Don't mind him," said Carl, "he never got over not making the freshman table tennis team at Crest View High."

"Now that was a low blow," said Jim. "It was actually the bowling team; at least get your story right! I hope you know I was just kidding, Trevor," said Jim.

"Oh, I'm sorry. For a second there I thought you were serious," said Trevor with a straight face, raising the concern of the group, and Jim, in particular. As Jim prepared to offer an apology, Trevor cut him off, "You mean you really were cut from the freshman table tennis team." With that, the group broke out into laughter.

Trevor used the levity of the group to transition back to a discussion of the survey results. "So, after you have the results of the focus group meetings, I would encourage you to refer to the **Six Elements of Gap Reduction** in developing your strategies for reducing the gaps that emerge as constants from the discussion," said Trevor.

"So, do I sense that you won't be helping us with that phase of this project?" Ed asked.

"Well, I didn't want to be presumptuous," said Trevor.

"Ok, let's talk about that once you finish with the focus groups, but for now, I will say that I don't see how we can go forward without your help," said Ed.

"Ditto," said Brenda, as the rest of the group nodded in agreement.

"I would be glad to assist in any way that I can," said Trevor.

Then Trevor placed the laser on the column, **Can't say**, and mentioned that often this response can represent a lack of knowledge about how the company aligns with the actions in the compass, and/or that the person isn't familiar with the compass as an action. "In any event, the task before you is to embed them in the culture so that they become clear practices that people are accountable to and can witness being practiced by others.

Three Reasons for Knowing and Building on Your Strengths

1. Knowing your strengths and applying them in a disciplined manner leads to a high level of evidentiary confidence.
2. Passion for your work emerges from having confidence in your abilities, knowledge, and ideas, which leads to an enjoyment of what you do and eventually a brand of excellence.
3. Having knowledge and confidence in your strengths leads to strategic thinking about leveraging your strengths to create opportunities in times of success that will give you a competitive advantage today, and in the future.

"Yeah, and I bet I know what you're going to say next," said Jim.

"What's that?" said Trevor.

"That we're the standard-bearers, the models for working and living by the values," replied Jim.

Trevor smiled and said, "Yep, you got that right! Moreover, if you can do that consistently, you'll transform this culture permanently. And that would be Swimming SidewayZ in a big way!"

Trevor turned off the LCD projector, put the laser pointer away, and asked the group if they had any questions.

"So, you and Brenda are all set with the next steps for getting started with the focus groups?" asked Ed.

"Yes, we're all set," said Brenda.

"Next week Trevor and I will be getting together over lunch to discuss logistics and meet with the department heads to decide which staff will be selected to participate in the meetings."

"I've mentioned to some of my people that we were going to be doing this and I was very pleased with the eagerness they showed for participating in the groups," said Carl. "Can we make suggestions about who should be included?" he continued.

"We are counting on it!" said Brenda. "As a matter of fact, we will be preparing a criterion for choosing participants so that the process has an element of objectivity and will be building in peer evaluations as well to ensure staff opinion is a part of the process."

"I like how you string the values through all of your activities," said Ed.

"I'm glad you perceived that," said Trevor, as he continued, "it's one of the things I try to model to my clients. If you can do that consistently you will have achieved a powerful way of keeping yourself aligned with the values as a leader."

"I hope we get more into this later in our work with you. I know I'm going to need some coaching in this area. The soft side isn't my strong suit," said Ed.

"Naugh!" said Jim, sarcastically. "No, seriously, I shouldn't joke about that. I'm sorry," said Jim, sensing the disfavor of the group.

"I commend you for being transparent about that," said Carl. "I will need a bit of work in this area myself. I was just being a butthead because I'm still learning to be transparent about my weakness and more so in asking for help. I appreciate that Ed, Jim, and Ben have been able to get past the fear of being vulnerable about their insecurities in our group."

"Thanks, Carl," said Jim, "that means a lot to me."

"No problem, bud!" said Jim.

Chapter 10

"Good morning, Trevor. Hi, this is Ed Preston. I hope I didn't wake you ... I'm sorry for calling you on a Sunday morning. Is this a good time to talk?"

"Yes, you didn't wake me. It's my allergies acting up; it's good to hear from you. What can I do for you?" asked Trevor cordially.

"Well, I wanted your opinion about something and please don't hesitate to speak your mind about it. I won't be offended in the least," said Ed sincerely.

"Well, thanks for letting me know Ed, but I sensed from the start of our work together that you were open to honest feedback. So, what is on your mind?"

"Well, I have a confession to make. In all the years I've managed, owned, and lead this company, I've never addressed the company as a whole," admitted Ed, apologetically.

Trevor was a bit surprised by Ed's statement and asked him how over more than twenty years he managed to grow the company so successfully without once speaking to the company.

Ed answered, "By bringing in others and staying the hell out of the way of my managers and supervisors. Besides, I have a real overwhelming fear of public speaking. I'm a master of one-on-one or small group communication, but I feel like I'm going to pass out in front of a large group. For a long time I was the only one bringing in large building accounts. I was used to doing business the way my uncle taught me to, with a handshake, and by keeping his distance from his workers. I made it clear to my executive staff what the goals and objectives were and left it up to them to meet with their respective staff. I was always taught to keep people on task, my dad and uncle always said time was money."

"You're saying more than that, Ed. You're telling me that the company has never come together in a company-wide meeting before ... not even for holidays and retirement parties, or to announce a company break- through?"

"Nope. All of those things have taken place, but within departments," said Ed, surprised by his own admittance.

"That's a first for me," said Trevor. In the worst run companies, leaders make public statements, even if it's to share bad news. What you're telling me is different from any organization I know. Now I have a better understanding of why Ben and the others were so proud of you for taking the risk of shifting to a more transparent and openly communicative style. Your decision is amazing in light of what you just revealed."

"It's nice of you to say that, but all I'm doing is following the instructions and admonition of the dolphins that saved my life."

"I see," said Trevor, in anticipation of Ed's next statement.

"As they were skipping backward on their fluke fins after pushing me onto the shore, they called out to me to Swim SidewayZ to escape Danger, to Change Bad Habits, and to Get Ahead. I'm trying to follow that advice, but it's hard at times. I mean, I'm working far outside of my comfort zone. Nevertheless, I can see the immediate benefits the change has produced with my executive group, so I'm truly committed to this change no matter how it turns out."

"It should turn out just fine," assured Trevor.

"Good, that leads me to my question. Do you think it would be a good idea for me to speak to the company tomorrow, prior to the focus group meetings?"

"Aaaahhh, well, yes, I mean, I think so."

"Forgive me Trevor, but you don't sound too sure."

"I'm sorry Ed; I'm just surprised given what you said a few minutes ago about your speaking anxiety."

"I've given a lot of thought to that as well; I was saved from the ocean and I feel that I owe it to my staff, myself, and the dolphins to break the chains of my fears and be all that I was saved to be. I guess you can say it feels somewhat like a calling, to be more of myself, to take advantage of my second chance," said Ed, viscerally.

Trevor, sensing the magnitude of the situation said, "That's great, Ed, what do you plan to talk about?"

"I thought I would tell the company the impetuous behind the organizational development work we're doing. I mean, share with them the story of how the dolphins saved my life and the lessons I learned that led me to change my leadership style."

Much to Ed's delight, Trevor said, "I think that's a fantastic idea! It will set the atmosphere for some awesome dialogue about the potential for change. I doubt what they suggest wouldn't be given every consideration after hearing such an honest life-changing story."

"Then we're all set. I will call the company together first thing in the morning and make my presentation. I will mention that I spoke with you today and that we agreed it would be a good idea for me to tell my story. Then, I'll call you and Brenda up to provide them an overview of what will take place over the next few days in the focus groups."

"That sounds good, Ed. Have you mentioned this to Brenda?"

"Not yet, I thought I would call her after I had a chance to bounce the idea off of you."

"Can you please have her call me so we can discuss what our roles will be?"

"Sure thing, and thanks for taking the time on a Sunday to speak with me."

"It was a pleasure; I'm on a cloud with this experience. While these developments are unprecedented at Preston, they are unique to me as well. The influence of the dolphins on you has transformed me too; I'm working in a consulting framework that no school or mentor could have taught me. It's one of the wondrous possibilities that life has to offer; thank you for allowing me to witness your courage and personal discoveries."

Ed called Brenda and relayed Trevor's request, informed her of his plan for speaking to the company, and asked her to announce his intentions to her staff. He then did the same with Carl, Ben, and Jim, who concluded his conversation with, "You are Swimming SidewayZ, Ed, you are Swimming SidewayZ, big fella!" This gave Ed cause to bellow with laughter.

The next morning the production floor was abuzz with wonder about what Ed was going to say. People were concerned that maybe it was bad news given the condition of the economy and the rumors prior to the Western deal. There was the possibility of layoffs; they pondered whether the deal had gone sour. Still, some thought it might be about Trevor, the stranger in their midst. While the department had mentioned what Trevor was doing with management, no one knew for sure what it all meant, or how it would eventually affect the company and its roles.

To manage his speaking anxiety, Ed looked down for the better part of the introduction of his talk, which began with a discussion of the truth about the financial condition of the company just a few weeks before the finalizing of the Western deal. As he began to tell of his adventure with the magical dolphins, particularly how they pleaded with him in English to Swim SidewayZ, he looked up and panned the room to find 500 people wide eyed, with mouths agape.

He proceeded with the conversation he had had with Anne and how she had assured him he had not lost his mind. He spoke about his research on the habits and values of the dolphins and his second chance to learn the lesson of Swimming SidewayZ. Moreover, he shared how the lessons he learned led him to tell this story to his management team.

He went on and spoke about the personal growth they all had experienced since he first told them about his encounter with the dolphins; how by practicing a leadership style of inclusion he empowered Ben to speak up and influence the owner of Western to place their business with us, and how that turned things around for the company. With that, the group let out a loud "atta-boy, Ben!" followed by thunderous applause. One of the women in Ben's department patted him on the back and gave him a wink of thanks and support.

Ed then spoke of how Brenda introduced the group to Trevor Bradshaw. He mentioned how he did an excellent job of helping them discover the values that they responded to in the survey, and how he and Brenda would be coming up soon to talk with them about the focus group meetings scheduled for the next couple of days.

Then Ed apologized to the group for waiting over twenty years to address them as a group. He spoke of how his parents and uncle taught him to solve problems by himself and to lead by example, and about his fear of public speaking. He said he owed them a great deal of thanks for all they had done over the years to make the company a success, in particular, his executive team who were surrogate heads of the company in his absence.

Then Jim shouted out, "You were never absent, Ed, we love you, man, and you're the best!"

Jim's acknowledgment was followed with loud applause by the group and chants of "Ed Preston, we love you, Ed Preston you're the best!"

When Ed heard those words, he began to weep softly through his words. Before his talk he thought he wasn't connected to these people, his insular approach to management had left that impossible. He was wrong; his commitment to preserving people's jobs in tough times and all that he had done for individuals and their families with giving them jobs and supporting them through various personal crises had made him their beloved. He just had not known it, now he couldn't deny it.

As Ed attempted to step away for Brenda and Trevor to address the group, Carl, Jim, and Ben broke into a chant of "Swimming SidewayZ, we're going to be Swimming SidewayZ!" Brenda and Trevor joined in, and before long, all 100 staff were chanting the phrase. It was clear Ed was smart to give the speech and Anne had been right as well. They did trust him and they did want his trust too.

When the chanting ended, Ed returned to the front of the room and spoke through applause as he told them Trevor would be working with the company to help it be a values centric company. In part, this meant that we would all be accountable to the values. He assured them he would address the company as a whole at least once a month in an attempt to be more transparent about the leadership of the company and to hear their voices on different issues.

As Ed moved away from the front of the room Brenda approached him misty eyed and shook his hand. As he stood to the side, his assistant whispered in his ear, "I had no idea you had that in you. If I had known your trip to the beach that afternoon was going to lead to all of this, I would have encouraged you to go swimming at midday on Fridays more often."

Ed looked at her, smiled, and said, "Well today is Thursday."

Chapter 11

Taking a sip of tea as he plucked a strawberry from his plate, Jim said, "Ok, give it to us straight," speaking to Brenda and Trevor as the group convened to debrief the morning after the focus group meetings.

"I couldn't be more pleased with the results of the meetings," said Brenda. Brenda was especially excited about the feedback she had received from the groups.

"I agree," said Trevor, "the groups were very clear and direct about what they thought and felt."

"Very good," said Ed.

Trevor stressed that he and Brenda were advocating a gradual approach to the task of reducing the gaps and leveraging the strengths discussed by the groups. They were taking this approach for the two reasons Brenda wrote on a flip chart.

"As you all know, I'm not a big fan of gradualism. If there was one area where I conflicted

1. To focus attention on no more than 3- 5 items that are most pertinent and critical to the company's ability to improve performance during the current economic crisis.

2. To ensure that the company works within its capacity, to achieve the goals; it must bring about the desired results it envisions based on the results from the focus

with my dad and uncle, it was the gradual way they approached change. I'm all for getting on with the task, but I'm not on this ship by myself, so I'm open to learning more about how gradualism can work in this situation," stated Ed.

"That's good to hear," said Brenda. "The only expeditious aspect of this process should be getting started with being gradual in learning how all this works and in what ways it will affect the company at every level."

"Well said," said Trevor.

"So it sounds like we'll be Swimming SidewayZ gradually," said Carl.

"Touché," said Jim.

Most of all, Brenda and Trevor were impressed with three central themes. Particularly the one about a compass supportive of the core value **"Teaming Together to Make Strategic Decisions"** that promotes striving to achieve healthy consensus in all collective decisions. Trevor explained that the theme: **"Feeling like an outsider"** was a very reflective opinion that was expressed by the majority of participants.

"That's interesting," said Ed, "but I think I understand where they are coming from. It's the reverse of the positive effects of diffusing the values, like in the fractal model, but in this case, it's analogous to how the management team felt excluded from my strategic decision making process, and how as a consequence duplicated this with their people. Is that close, I mean, does that make sense?"

"You nailed that one," said Trevor.

"Wow, so my people think that I don't include them in decision making," said Ben, contritely.

"Not exactly, Ben," said Brenda. "They feel included. I mean, we're doing a good job of asking questions and getting their input, but we need to take it a step further, as we discussed earlier, and allow them to assist in shaping the decisions through consensus. Essentially, we need not dominate the process as much as we need to encourage more challenging dialogue and hear more sides of an issue."

"Yes, and be comfortable with decisions that are not our own," said Jim.

"Yep, I'm guilty of that myself," said Carl.

"Me, too," said Brenda.

"Well, don't feel bad about this," said Trevor, "making all the decisions is encouraged and often intoxicating when leaders experience the level of success Preston has enjoyed. People seldom complain when their pockets are full."

"That's a fact," said Brenda, "I surely never complained to Ed. We were all keeping our opinions to ourselves until Ed made his leadership shift. I'm glad we got that on the table; where do we go from here, Ed."

"The first step is doing some training and coaching of the management team on building consensus in groups and passing that knowledge onto the supervisors, with me observing people applying the skills in real time."

"That sounds like a smart approach."

"Thank you, Ed," said Trevor. "To save costs, Brenda and I agreed that I would train her and her staff and they would conduct the training and coaching.

"I like that a lot, thanks for being sensitive to our financial situation, Trevor," said Carl.

"Yeah, I was wrong about you fella, you're all right," said Jim, jokingly.

The second theme Brenda wanted to discuss involved a compass supportive of the core value, **"Unselfish Concern for Others" (We promote and celebrate the achievements and best efforts of others.)** Focus group members were interested in forming a recognition and rewards committee of peers who would develop and rate people's performance against the perceptions of internal and external stakeholders. Trevor told the groups that it was a brilliant idea and a program he has implemented in other companies. What he suggested to the groups was to limit the evaluations to living the values, not the technical aspect of performance. He explained that was an area that should be left to management, as there were too many aspects of a person's job that were either unknown to others, or outside their scope of understanding. "That's a real interesting approach to recognizing people," said Ben.

"What do you mean by interesting?" Said Trevor, "I'm just wondering what management's role will be in this and how will it affect my ability to do performance evaluations."

As Trevor began to answer Ben, Brenda interjected, "May I, Trevor?"

"Sure," said Trevor.

"I wanted to respond to your question, Ben, because I've been working on a new performance evaluation system that will integrate seamlessly with this idea. It's called a **'Total Score Card.'** Basically, the objective is to expand our evaluation method to include the core values and opinions of others in other departments and our external stakeholders.

The recognition and rewards committee could contribute to this process by providing management with the data they collect from staff. Ultimately, we would be responsible for conducting an evaluation of our people, but imagine how much more objective the process would be with the inclusion of the data committee members will provide."

"I will need to see how this will work, but I like the idea of the total score card. We need to have a way of recognizing and rewarding people for living by the values. In addition, it would enrich the evaluation by expanding the organizational areas we should be assessing," said Trevor.

"That is real solid stuff; I can get behind that idea," said Ben.

"Me, too," said Carl, "but what about teaching the values to people. It just seems like we need to get a bit more formal in structuring a way of teaching how we align with the technical side of the job."

"You folks are starting to scare me a bit with the rate by which you're starting to move ahead with this strategy of living by values," said Trevor.

Then he continued, "When we enter the management training portion of the work, we'll learn the **M.O.G.S.** system, which is an approach to managing by values. I developed this approach a few years ago while consulting with clients in the food service industry. The acronym stands for "**Management Observation and Growth System**."

1. It illuminates the connective points between duties and responsibilities.

2. It introduces the importance of reciprocity in strengthening relationships and strategies for maintaining in order to build engagement for organizational health and productivity.

M.O.G.S. is a hybrid tool that empowers managers with the ability to lead by values, through a values driven approach, consisting of a six-step strategy: **Orientation, Training, Coaching, Evaluation, Delegation/Mentorship, and Followership**.

"What feature about M.O.G.S. excites you the most?" asked Jim, quizzically.

"Actually, there are two things that I'm enthusiastic about," said Trevor, as he gestured to Brenda to toss him a marker. He wrote his responses on the flip chart.

"Those sound like some very novel concepts, Trevor," said Jim.

"Yes, they're for organizations that have yet to be introduced to them. Those who have experience great results and enjoy measurable increases in productivity and morale in ways that are self-sustaining."

The third theme that Brenda and Trevor wanted to discuss involved a compass supportive of the core value, "**Trust starts with allowing for mistakes**." We promote an environment of career-long learning by supporting the right to learn from our mistakes that are the results of earnest efforts.

"The belief that productivity and morale would be higher if there were more opportunities to learn from mistakes was a prevalent topic during discussions in all the groups," said Trevor, as Brenda nodded her head in agreement.

Making eye contact with Brenda, Ed asked, "Are we saying that we want to be an organization that accepts people making mistakes; I have a hard time believing we can stay in business making mistakes. Why not be a company that encourages people to get things right? I mean, do we want to Swim SidewayZ to this degree?"

"Yeah, I share Ed's opinion. I wouldn't want to buy windows from the company that prides itself on making mistakes. I mean, imagine if Ben had told the CEO of Western that what made us different from the competition was our ability to make mistakes," said Jim.

"Interesting you would say that," said Trevor, "because it was exactly the realization that the CEO had learned from Ben, that he was making the mistake of choosing vendors based on the single criterion of cost, which influenced him to choose in our favor. If he wasn't open to learning from his mistake, he may have tuned Ben out."

Jim listened to Trevor but remained puzzled.

Sensing Jim's confusion, Brenda chimed in, "The relationship between productivity and morale in relation to creating an environment where people are allowed to make mistakes can be understood by imagining how difficult it would be for a child to learn something if a parent scolded him every time he got it wrong. Yes, even under strong scrutiny, the child can sometimes manage to get it right. However, this is at the cost of the child experiencing anxiety, self-doubt, and low confidence, all of which will affect his ability and willingness to engage the parent and/or the task(s) in the future."

Hearing Brenda's example, the folds in Jim's forehead relaxed a bit. Nevertheless, sensing Ed's reluctance, Trevor contributed an allegory that sat close to home. "When Ed was stuck struggling in the rip current, he made the mistake of swimming harder in the belief that it would get him to shore. When he failed to make progress towards the shore his effort changed to trying even harder, thus he made the same mistake twice. Moreover, what did he learn?" asked Trevor, rhetorically, "that he was using the wrong approach? He also learned that he didn't have an alternative strategy. Witnessing his peril, his dolphin friends approached him with an innovative concept, to Swim SidewayZ out of the current. Ed's response was to make yet a third mistake, to ignore the advice of his friends and go with the strategy of accepting his impending demise."

As Trevor spoke, a soft smile and a sparkle came to Ed's face. "Living according to ancient dolphin values, teamwork, and unselfish concern for others, the dolphins rescued Ed and encouraged him to learn from his mistake. Where would we be if the dolphins were intolerant of mistakes … and Anne, Ed's wife, where would she be?"

With tears in his eyes, Ed acknowledged that he understood the value of learning from mistakes as a compass. "Trevor, thanks for that anecdote. As I told Brenda recently, it's going to be a while before I completely shift my thinking. Just when I think I've bought in, I find myself on a slippery slope again; will I ever get full traction? I'm afraid that I won't be an acceptable standard-bearer?"

"You'll be fine," assured Trevor.

"Thanks, but how can you be so sure?" asked Carl, reflecting on his own anxieties.

"I know because he can feel the pain of not fulfilling his expectations and because of his willingness to be repentant and accountable. What you're witnessing in Ed is what all leaders' who are successful at living by values go through."

"What is that?" asked Jim cautiously.

"In the process of transformation, a leader will always experience some sort of painful breaking away from old styles of thinking before accepting new ones that empower him to live by values. The successful ones at some point learn to recognize the elements associated with this change and allow the elements to unfold in their consciousness." Trevor went to the flip chart and wrote the seven elements of transformation that successful leaders experience when they embrace living by values as a leadership style.

Trevor's list prompted Ed to speak. "I really appreciate this list. It gives me a way to think about the experience I'm having adjusting to the idea of living by values, especially the notion that courageousness will always be necessary. I was expecting some immediate and definite outcome to this process. I now know that was a mistake; no pun intended. I understand it will be a day-to-day challenge and without allowing myself to learn from my mistakes, I won't stand a chance of learning to live by the values."

"Me too. I understand the power of Ed's dream; it gave him another chance to learn from his mistake and to try again at getting it right. It was all about teaching him to allow others to learn from their mistakes."

"Even I can't argue with that," said Jim.

"It sounds as if you all would benefit from having an emblem to remind you that you have the capability to Swim SidewayZ through your feelings of self-doubt about living according to your values. In the interim of us reconvening to implement the values, give some thought to a symbolized representative of the values that could serve as a reminder of all that has transpired since Ed shared his story with you," asserted Trevor.

Seven Elements of Leadership Transformation

1. I'm not perfect
2. People are not a means, but a part of my success
3. People are never the problem
4. Reciprocity is essential for healthy relationships
5. Courage will always be necessary
6. Accountability and transparency empower people to be honest mirrors in our lives
7. I recognize a need for change

"I like it! We could build on Brenda's idea and put a poster in every office and the reception area," said Ben.

Trevor told the group they could superimpose the values on a poster of the emblem to reinforce the significance of the relationship between them.

As soon as he said this, Ed remembered what he had written down about the significance of the "Z" in the word SidewayZ, and grabbed a marker. He went to the flip chart, drew a large "Z," and told the group that that was his contribution to developing an emblem.

The team asked him to remind them what the "Z" stood for. He told them that the "Z" was a reminder of what the dolphins had taught him: "To Swim SidewayZ through the strong currents of life and business and to teach others to do the same thing."

The group paused and Jim said, "I think we should offer the company an opportunity to vote on this, but, in homage to the dolphins that gave us this wisdom and saved your life, I say let's go with it."

"I think it makes perfect sense since we're spelling the word with a Z," encouraged Carl.

"I think it would be crazy not to use it, and I can't imagine our people not supporting it after hearing Ed's story," insisted Brenda.

With Brenda's endorsement of the emblem, the group also agreed on the three values they would focus on and then follow-up on with management.

Ed suggested that he would share the idea of the "Z" and the three values at the next all-company meeting in two weeks. The group agreed it was a great idea. Trevor asked the group if they had any takeaways from the meeting before they adjourned.

Jim immediately spoke up, "I haven't been totally transparent about my feelings during this process." The group grew a bit tense as Jim spoke.

"Please speak your mind, Jim. I'm glad you feel comfortable with living out the values in this way," said Ed, as he braced himself.

"Well, um, you see, ah. This has been an extraordinarily beautiful experience for me. It has already led me to function differently at home. My wife and children told me the other day, whatever it means, by all means, keep Swimming SidewayZ!"

The group broke into laughter as Ed walked across the room and gave Jim a big hug.

Trevor discussed next steps for working with the group on developing the values-centric model. He mentioned that he would be meeting with Ed and Brenda to set up a schedule for training Brenda and her team. Coaching the group in the methods, processes, and skills necessary for integrating the values into their leadership/management approach will happen after the training they received from Brenda and her team.

Trevor told the group it had been a real pleasure working with them on this phase of the project and wished them a splendid weekend.

As the group left the room, Trevor packed up his equipment, markers, and flip charts. In the process he looked up and saw Ed standing in the doorway. "Yes, Ed?" said Trevor, lifting his eyebrows.

"After you finish packing your things I was hoping to chat with you a bit as you walked out to your car."

As Trevor approached Ed in the doorway, Ed took the flip chart from Trevor. "Here, let me help you with that. My father used to say, 'don't just stand there, lend a hand.'"

As they walked into the parking lot Ed said, "I wanted to ask you a question; you're an organizational psychologist, right?"

"Yes," said Trevor.

"Does that make you qualified to work with leaders on a one-on-one basis? I mean, I think I need some quality time with you to get at some issues that have surfaced sense you began working with us."

"Anything you need to speak about immediately?" said Trevor.

"Not really, it's nothing heavy, it's not like I need a shrink or anything, I just would like to address some issues related to my need to control every detail of my business. I'm bit afraid that I won't succeed at delegating the work to others."

"I see," said Trevor. "Well, I recall you telling me that a turning point for you in revealing the dolphin story was the encouragement Anne gave you to trust yourself with your people. They needed to know that you trusted them."

"Wow, you're good. I mean, you remembered that!"

"Sure I did. When people tell their stories to me I honor every detail as a witness and a mirror into their lives. When you speak to me, it's like hearing your echo in a canyon, you get to hear your message twice," said Trevor, with a smile.

"Ok, connect the dots for me. What does Anne's encouragement have to do with my concern around delegating?"

Turning from putting his equipment into the trunk of his car, Trevor turned and looked Ed straight in the eyes. "Delegating is a form of empowerment. If you're comfortable with empowering people you trust, you will learn to delegate to them under the right conditions. However, you must be clear that you understand the task and your expectations. When you spoke to Anne about your confusion and caution about addressing your staff's trust issues, you were empowering her to help you think through the problem. You understood she was a resource who was knowledgeable about the challenges you faced managing your introversion and need for control. You decided to empower Anne because you had a lot of experience following her advice. Now you need to give yourself a chance to learn through a process of empowering and delegating to build trust with your ability to recognize the conditions that warrant empowerment and delegation. It won't come as magically as your dolphin experience, but it will emerge."

"I'm glad you believe that," said Ed, as Trevor opened the driver-side door.

"I would love to chat further Ed, but I have a tennis date with my wife and I don't want to have to Swim SidewayZ through L.A. traffic, so I'd better get going. I'll call you Monday to set up a one-on-one meeting session for us," said Trevor.

"Ok, I'll look forward to speaking with you. I appreciate you taking the time to speak with me now. Tell your wife it was my fault you were late."

"Don't think I won't," said Trevor, chuckling as he sped off.

Ed decided to stop for the day. It was Friday, and he decided to call his assistant from the car and tell her he was not returning to the office. As he drove home he approached the beachfront home of his friend and decided to drop by for a visit. He called ahead but no one answered, so he decided to take a walk on the beach. As he strolled along the shore, he looked out over the ocean where he had met his magical friends. As he stared far into the horizon, he saw three figures somersaulting in synchronicity and he reflected on the gift he had received.

Reflections and Action-Step Guide

Chapter 1

Are you denying any miracles in your life or business? If yes, what are they?

_____

_____

_____

_____

What does Swimming SidewayZ mean in your life?

_____

_____

_____

_____

What must you do differently in your life or business in order to get ahead?

_____

_____

_____

_____

Chapter 2

What areas in your professional or personal life would benefit from you Swimming SidewayZ?

Professional Areas

_____

_____

_____

Personal Areas

_____

_____

_____

What goals should you set?

_____

_____

_____

What strategies do you need to employ?

_____

_____

_____

Chapter 3

Are there any gaps in your relationships with people in your professional or personal life? Yes or No (Circle one). If yes, please explain below.

_____

_____

_____

_____

Describe the Professional Relational Gap(s)

_____

_____

_____

_____

What are the consequences?

_____

_____

_____

_____

What is the strategy for reducing the gap(s)?

_____

_____

_____

_____

What are the benefits and how can they be used to strengthen your relationships?

_____

_____

_____

_____

Chapter 4

In what way do you need to Swim SidewayZ personally or professionally in order to achieve your life or career goals?

_____

_____

_____

_____

What challenges do you anticipate with the change?

_____

_____

_____

_____

What resources will you deploy to help you to meet the challenges?

_____

_____

_____

_____

How will you and others benefit?

_____

_____

_____

_____

Chapter 5

What are your personal and/or core business values?

_____

_____

_____

_____

What opportunities to live out your personal or business values are you missing?

_____

_____

_____

_____

Chapter 6

Does your organization and/or personal performance and conduct align with your values? Yes or No (Circle one). If no, please explain below.

_____

_____

_____

_____

How would you describe your readiness for change in order to fulfill your personal or organizational mission, vision, values, and goals?

_____

_____

_____

_____

What challenges must you overcome to fulfill your personal or organizational mission, vision, values, and goals?

_____

_____

_____

_____

Chapter 7

How would you describe your behavior and/or that of your organization during periods of great success? Would you say that you were more or less aligned with its core values? Please explain.

How would you describe your behavior and/or that of your organization during periods of poor performance? Would you say that you or the organization, or both, were more aligned with its core values? Please explain.

Chapter 8

Share about one or two of your own values experiences.

_____

_____

_____

_____

What have you learned from the values experiences of
others in your professional or personal life?

_____

_____

_____

_____

Chapter 9

In what areas of your professional or personal life are you experiencing challenges with transparency?

_____

_____

_____

_____

How has practicing transparency benefited you and those in your professional or personal life?

_____

_____

_____

_____

Chapter 10

How much quality time do you spend with the people who contribute to your personal and professional success?

_____

_____

_____

_____

What personal challenges or perspectives do you have that may be preventing you from being more engaged with the people who contribute to your success?

_____

_____

_____

_____

Chapter 11

What three values-alignment issues in your personal or professional life require your immediate attention?

_____

_____

_____

_____

What strategies do you have for recognizing people who have contributed to your success or happiness?

_____

_____

_____

_____

What challenges do you face with being courageous as a leader and how are you working to overcome them?

_____

_____

_____

_____

~NOTES~

THE SWIM SIDEWAYZ TEAM

Dr. Robert Watts, Jr. (Author)

Dr. Watts is an organizational consultant, executive coach, organizational leader, teacher, speaker, and author of the acclaimed books *People Are Never the Problem – Refuse to Play the Blame Game,* and *The Development of L.A.D.S. (Learning Analysis Diagnosis Solution) Model.* His powerful speaking topics and skills as a storyteller and presenter have audiences calling him America's Best Kept Secret! Watts is the founder and Chief Solution Officer of Watts and Associates, an organizational development-consulting firm in Central California.

Prior to becoming an acclaimed author and speaker, Watts thrilled audiences with his athletic excellence as an All-American football player at Boston College and in the National Football League with the New Orleans Saints and the Oakland Raiders.

Robert Watts, III (Illustrator)

Robert is the senior half of the brother and sister team that produced the illustrations and book cover for Swim SidewayZ. In 2010, the Oakland California branch of the YWCA presented the first exhibit of Robert's artwork during Black History Month. His artwork can also be viewed at his website: www.thirdgenerationstudios.com. When he is not creating art, Robert works as the Program Manager for the Teens on Target program at Youth ALIVE!, a non-profit public health agency dedicated to preventing youth violence and generating youth leadership.

Erika R. Watts (Illustrator)

Erika is the other half of the brother sister team that produced the illustrations and book cover for Swim SidewayZ. Erika attended the San Francisco Academy of Art for one year before transferring to the American Conservatory of Theatre in San Francisco, California.

ABOUT THE AUTHOR

Dr. Robert Watts Jr. was born and raised in New York. He attended public school in New York city and at the age of fifteen accepted a special grant to attend Vermont Academy in Saxton River, Vermont. While at VA, he excelled in sports, earning All-Prep honors in track and field, football, and basketball. In his senior year, he captained both the football and basketball teams to undefeated seasons. He was also a recipient of the coveted Voice Literary Award for poetry.

In 1973, Robert entered Boston College on a football scholarship. As a freshman and sophomore, he played tight end for the Eagles. In his junior year, he switched to linebacker where he made the All-Eastern College Team and All-American his senior year.

In 1977, he was drafted by the New Orleans Saints in the third round of the NFL draft. Spinal injuries cut his career short, but not before he had a chance to play for the Oakland Raiders in 1978.

In 1997, he was inducted into the Boston College Varsity Club Hall of Fame. He was also named an honorary member of the Vermont Academy Board of Trustees.

In 1983, he was inducted into the Vermont Academy Sports Hall of Fame. With his football career over at the age of twenty-six, Robert entered graduate school at San Francisco State University and in 1986 earned a master's degree in Speech and Communication Studies. He returned to school in 2005 to fulfill a dream interrupted by a bout with cancer in 1989, and earned his doctorate in the psychology of organizational development from Alliant International University.

For inquiries write to:
Dr. Robert Watts Jr., Watts & Associates
P.O. Box 0755
Clovis, California 93612-0755
or
www.robertwattsjr.com

Additional copies of this book
are available from your
local bookstore
or through the following media:
e-books
www.robertwattsjr.com

Watts & Associates
Clovis, California